Tarnished Knight: A London Steampunk Novella

Cover Art © Damonza

To obtain permission to excerpt portions of the text, please contact the
author at www.becmcmaster.com

❋ Created with Vellum

"The Mech Who Loved Me has everything I've come to expect from McMaster: compelling characters, **sizzling sexual tension**, mystery, danger, and of course, true love." - *Let Them Read Books Blog*

"Richly imagined, gritty and dark, and **full of hot heroes and hot sex**... utterly delicious. " – *Smart Bitches, Trashy Books* **for** *Kiss of Steel*

"Action, adventure...and **blazing hot seduction**...Bec McMaster offers it all." -**Eve Silver, author of** *Sins of the Flesh* **for** *Kiss of Steel*

Kiss Of Steel—Georgia RWA Maggies Best Paranormal Romance 2013

Heart Of Iron—One of Library Journal's Best Romances 2013 and nominated for RT Reviews Best Steampunk 2013

Forged By Desire—RITA Finalist Paranormal Romance 2015

Of Silk And Steam—RT Reviews Best Steampunk Romance 2016 and SFR Galaxy Award winner

Mission: Improper—#1 Amazon Steampunk Bestseller

To Catch A Rogue—RITA Finalist Paranormal Romance 2019

Nobody's Hero—Two-time SFR Galaxy Awards winner

The Last True Hero—Dark Paranormal PRISM winner 2018

Hexbound—Historical Fantasy PRISM winner 2017

Soulbound—Historical Fantasy PRISM winner 2018 and overall PRISM Best of the Best

TARNISHED KNIGHT

BEC MCMASTER

CHAPTER 1

"*R*ight this way, guv."

The boy hurried ahead of Rip, his roughened boots churning the snow and mud to sludge. He kept darting a glance over his shoulder, fully aware of exactly what stalked behind him.

John 'Rip' Doolan strode through the cold streets behind the lad with his hands thrust into the pockets of his heavy coat.

The fingers on his left hand kept twitching, trying to stir some semblance of heat into the limb. Of the right, all he could feel was the heavy pull of the hydraulics in his forearm as the mech hand flexed. Rough work. Rookery work. But it served its purpose. Though the aristocratic Echelon that ruled London city considered him less of a man because of it – less than human – he couldn't run this line of work without two feasible limbs.

Jem Saddler paused at the intersection ahead, blowing into his cupped palms. The work-chafed fingers struck through the end of his gloves. The boy'd lost one the year previous, when the biting cold came in. Not uncommon in

Whitechapel, where flats and tenements slumped against each other like slatterns on a winter's night, seeking warmth against the bitter chill. Few here had coin enough to keep the fires burning all night and from the neat little slash that gaped in the fabric beneath the boy's arm, the coat had once belonged to someone else. Clothing was hard to come by too, except for the more enterprising.

Rip's eyes narrowed as he surveyed Petticoat Lane and the alleys off it. The ever-present ropes that slung between the upper stories of the alleys were bare of the ghostly flap of laundry. Fire burned in a barrel on the corner and a pair of dollymop's huddled around it, warming their hands. One of them eyed him warily, a frozen little smile etching itself onto her lips. Coin was coin, but he knew what he looked like. Wouldn't be the first time a woman hoped he walked away.

"Where's the 'ouse?" Rip asked, turning to Jem and pretending he didn't notice her sigh of relief.

"Down there," Jem replied, pointing at a narrow laneway that ran between buildings. "It's Liza Kent's place. She ain't been seen near on three days. Thought 'er old man might 'ave given 'er the touch-up, but no sniff o' 'im either."

Rip tugged a pair of shillings from his pocket and flipped them toward the lad. "You done good. Keep your eyes and ears open and there'll be more o' the ready where that came from."

Jem snatched the pair of coins out of the air like a conjurer and grinned.

"Liza's flash gent touch 'er up much?" It weren't none of his business but the hair on the back of Rip's neck rose as the darkness within him stirred. Memory reared its ugly head; his mother staggering back into the stove as her pimp laid into her with his fists. Rip had been small then, powerless. He wasn't powerless anymore, and there was nothing he despised more than a man who raised his hand to a woman.

Jem must have sensed the slither of darkness inside him for he swallowed. "No more'n usual, guv."

Easy. Rip squeezed his eyes shut and forced the yearning hunger in him to subside. Six months of living with the hot, gut-twisting clench of it; he was starting to recognize what set it off and how to avoid that.

Becoming a blue blood with their unnatural thirst for blood wouldn't have been his choice, if there'd been one. Six months ago though, a vampire had torn his throat open and half disembowelled him. He could remember the hot-wet splash of his own blood as pain washed through him like brandy-soaked flames. Lying on the roof, his heels drumming on the tiles as he coughed wetly into the night. And then his master, Blade, leaning over him with a desperate whisper. *"We're gonna give you me blood. The virus might keep you 'live long enough to 'eal your wounds."*

He knew what it meant. Blade had asked before if he wanted to become a blue blood. In their dark little world, the threat of death or crippling injury was a constant and the craving virus could heal anything short of decapitation. Still, he'd always said no before.

Until Blade whispered the one little thing that might have changed his mind. *"If you don't want it, blink. If you do, squeeze me fingers. But know that this'll devastate Esme."*

Esme. Christ. In that moment he'd seen a flash of her serious face, with the slashing dark wings of her brows, and Rip couldn't have said no despite himself. He'd always kept his distance but the sudden hot flare of yearning – the urge to see her just once more – was too strong for him. And so he'd squeezed Blade's hand.

The next he knew he was flat on his back in his own bed, with Esme straddling his hips, her firm, no-nonsense fingers going to the buttons at her throat. The other half of the equation began to sink in. Blood. And as soon as he realized what she was there for, a fierce aching *need* had burned through him like white-hot fire, draining away the colour from his vision until all he could smell was the violet water on her skin and see the heady tick of her pulse in her throat. Hands on her, yanking her close. And Blade holding him back. *"Easy now, lad. You don't want to frighten 'er, do* you?"

The craving virus had healed him all right. But he'd never thought about the other edge of the coin. The fierce hunger he could barely control. Especially around her.

"You don't need me no more?" Jem asked somewhat nervously and Rip realized he'd been staring.

He gave a rough shake of his head. "I'll check on it."

The lad tossed him a tremulous smile, then bolted back along the street.

Hands in his pockets and his shoulders hunched, Rip began to cross the street, slipping in the wet slush. The scent of roasting chestnuts drifted past and raucous laughter sounded nearby. Someone had hung a bedraggled strand of holly in their window. Christmas, he remembered suddenly. Nearly upon them.

Not the sort of thing the blue bloods of the Echelon celebrated, since the Church had excommunicated them, but it lingered in the human remnants of the population. Almost a defiant gesture in fact. The Echelon might have burned the churches in England and arrested any caught praying or on consecrated ground, but they couldn't police everything.

Nor could they arrest half of London.

The laughter wasn't quite enough to hush the almost silent footstep that followed him. Rip glanced down beneath his lashes, a shiv sliding into his hand. He kept it tucked against the heavy cup of his palm, hiding it low against his thigh. As he turned the corner, stepping into the shadowed alcove of the alley, he pressed his back against the wall and waited.

The shadow behind him lengthened and Rip stepped forward, slashing out with the blade. He caught a hint of musk in his nose and pulled the blow, snarling under his breath. "Bloody 'ell."

A hand caught his wrist. Rip glared up into the unnatural golden eyes of a tall youth, tempted for one moment to push back. But that was the hunger in him, the fury. And if he pushed too far, he knew who would end this fight the victor.

Not even a blue blood could take on a verwulfen without consequences. In the strange berserker furies that overtook them they were practically invincible.

Will shoved away. "What are you doin' here?"

"I ought ask you the same question." Rip sheathed the shiv, anger a slow-burn in his blood. He knew the answer of course. Blade must have sent Will to watch him. Make sure he didn't lose control in the middle of the rookery and spill blood on the dirty gleam of the icy slush. A shiver ran down his spine, his mouth watering. *Tempting. Just to give in, just once...*

"Thought you might need a hand," Will muttered, heat burnishing his cheeks. He hadn't expected to get caught.

"Aye," Rip said, flexing the steel grip of his fingers. "You're about ten years too late."

A faint smile curled over the young man's mouth. Then Will stepped past, nostrils flaring as he surveyed the alley. "What you up to?"

"Jem Saddler said Liza Kent ain't been sighted near on three days. No sign o' 'er old man neither," Rip replied, falling into place beside him.

Will stopped outside a wooden door, eyeing the painted symbol of a pair of crossed daggers above the lintel. The matching tattoo was branded on the inside of Rip's wrist. A sign of ownership, of protection. Blade's mark. Will's nostrils flared again.

"What you smellin'?" Rip asked. His own senses had increased since he'd changed, but Will could smell what a man had for breakfast three days prior.

"Strange." Will frowned, his enormous shoulders bunching beneath the oiled canvas of his coat as he stepped forward. He pressed his fingertips against the door. "Chemical," he said. "But nothin' else. Smells like Honoria's laboratory."

Blade's new wife. Rip breathed in deeply, finding a faint trace of the vinegary tang that reminded him of the laboratory. Pushing open the door, he frowned when it gave way easily. Unlocked.

Not even the most desperate thief would cross a threshold with Blade's mark on it. Still... This was Whitechapel.

"Hullo?" Rip called, his voice echoing through the room. He knew the place was empty before he'd even taken a step. The cold was biting here; the chill emptiness of a place that hadn't been occupied in some days. His hard gaze raked the room. A frying pain in the wash basin, a pile of darning in the corner... Someone had dragged a thin curtain over the doorway separating this from the bedroom beyond and suddenly Rip could smell it.

Blood.

He yanked the curtain open. A man lay spread-eagled on the thin mattress, his torso slit from chest to groin and intestines spilling out like raw sausages. The blood was long since dried, the scent still strangely diluted. Rip's swallowed hard as his vision dipped, painting the world in shadows of grey and white. He almost had it under control when Will brushed against his shoulder and suddenly he *could* smell something; blood, hot and fresh, pumping beneath the other man's skin.

Rip shoved past, staggering out into the alley. He'd fed the day before, but obviously not enough. The world spun around him, the chestnut vendor's laughter grating against his skin. His head turned that way, the predator in him tracking the man by sound alone.

Hell. Rip shook his head hard, his fumbling fingers dragging a cheroot from his pocket and a packet of matches. He lit it hastily, knowing from the listening sound of the silence behind him that Will was watching.

"You all right?"

"Fine," he snapped, raking his metal hand over the back of his neck. It was better out here. Not so close. The sounds from the street nearby made it harder to pick out the rushing throb of blood through Will's veins.

Will stepped off the porch, his boots sloshing through the snow-melt. "Did a right number on him. We ought to tell Blade."

Rip's fingers tightened on the cheroot. "No. Let 'im be." This was the Warren's first Christmas and Blade was determined to make it a special one for Honoria. He had enough to manage. "I'll deal with it."

Even if only to prove to himself that he could. Rip'd been nigh on useless the last six months. Too stricken by the hunger to be of much good to anyone. He had to prove that he could control it and this was his best chance. Tossing the cheroot on the cobbles, Rip ground it into the wet sludge and started for the street.

"Call me if you need me," Will muttered.

Rip shoved his hands into his pockets and caught the eye of the whore near the fire barrel. His mouth watered as he jerked his chin at her. Time to take care of one need at least. So he could start thinking on who'd killed Liza Kent's old man, and where the hell she'd gone.

THE FIRST COLD kiss against Esme's cheek made her look up. Soft flakes of snow tumbled from the stormy sky, tangling in the black strands of her hair. Her hands tightened around the basket in her hands. She'd always loved snow. When she'd first come to the 'Chapel after her husband Tom died, she'd despised the grim tenements and filthy hovels. For nearly a year she'd managed to scrape enough coin together to barely feed herself, until a too-friendly neighbour had made it clear that he could find other work for her... if she was willing to lie on her back. She'd hated the world then, hated the rookery. When she first went to Blade and begged for protection in exchange for her blood, he'd frightened her as much as the rest of the world had.

Only when the snows had come, washing away the grimness and painting the world in a feathery white, had she come to see any sign of joy or laughter in this dark world. Blade had been patient with her, offering her a position as his housekeeper when it became clear she was so frightened of the blood-letting that she could barely stand it at first. Even the grim men who worked for him had begun to terrify her less as she grew to know them. Tin Man with the thin metal sheeting over his scalp and his inability to speak; Will, the feral verwulfen boy who Blade had rescued from life in a cage and Rip, whom she'd almost fainted in front of when she first saw the broad-shouldered giant.

In his own quiet way, he'd won her trust the most, soothing her with his deep voice and helping her with her chores. He'd never asked for anything in return for his help and gradually she'd realised he never would. That more than anything had made her start trusting men again.

Though he worked as one of Blade's enforcers Rip was so gentle with her, as if even he feared his strength. And he had a sense of humour so dry that it often took her a moment to realise he'd made a joke. Then that slow smile would spread over his face, catching her breath in her chest and warming parts of her that missed her husband. He was her friend, and only that, though she was the first to admit that she longed for more.

She'd slowly become accustomed to the world she lived in over the years. Accepting her role as Blade's housekeeper and even as his blood thrall. Before Honoria had arrived, of course. Blade drank his blood cold now, out of respect for his wife and Esme... Well, she was waiting.

A man stepped out of the shadows ahead, watching her. Esme's lips curved in a genuine smile as she saw Will. He noticed her of course, his amber eyes roving the streets with a predatory interest. Men moved out of his way as he tipped his chin up and smiled at her, ignoring them. He'd been bigger than everyone else ever since he'd arrived in the rookery as a boy. Most people saw that as dangerous but Esme knew better. Will was verwulfen – of course he was dangerous – but he was also fiercely protective and that protection had always extended to her.

"Will!" She held out her gloved hand and he offered her his arm. The move was awkward but well-intentioned. Even through the thick oilskin of his coat she could feel the unnatural heat of his skin and the hint of tension in the thick muscles of his forearm.

Esme looked up. "What's wrong?"

"Nothin'."

"William Carver," she scolded. "I may not have your hearing or your sense of smell, but I know when you're lying to me."

Will rubbed a rough hand over the back of his neck, a flush of red darkening his high cheekbones. "Come. I'll walk you home." A faint, almost Scottish burr corrupted the words, a sure sign that he was nervous or upset. He rarely showed any signs of his birth country now.

Esme planted her feet as he tried to steer her down the street. Away from the nearby alley. He *was* hiding something.

Tugging free–though in effect he let her go–Esme strode to the mouth of the alley and peered down it curiously.

There was a couple pressed against the pitted brick wall. The whore's skirt was tucked up as a sign of availability; her profession's calling card. Tangled blonde hair tumbled down her back as she threw her head back with a gasp, the long smooth column of her throat gleaming pale in the cold after-noon light. Her arms curled up around the man's back, her nails biting into the thick muscle of his shoulder blades. Unconsciously, the woman pressed against him, her hips grinding against his as if it felt good, so good–and the part of Esme that had once been Blade's thrall knew exactly how that felt. Blood fired through her body, a hot flush of need. Then she saw the metal gleaming as rough steel fingers slid up the woman's nape, clenching in her hair as he held her still. The familiar blunt features; some would have even called them terrifying. She had, once upon a time. Before she knew him. Before she saw something different every time she looked at him.

Rip.

His mouth trailing over the woman's throat, lips still glis-tening with blood. Heat rushed out of Esme's face and down her neck, as if her heart was constricting in her chest and drawing all of the blood in her body into a small, clenched fist beneath her lungs. She took a step back and stumbled on something. A paper bag of garbage strewn in the streets. Catching her balance, she saw Rip's head jerk up sharply, the all-consuming blackness of his pupils drowning out the colour of his irises. As if coming out of a daze his gaze locked on her, those diamond-sharp eyes boring through her. A harsh breath tore through his throat, his body rocking on the balls of his feet as if for one moment he made to move toward her.

"Rip," the whore whispered, sliding a possessive hand up his throat and turning his face back to hers. She shivered and gave a breathy little laugh. "That feels amazin'. Never thought I'd say it, but you want more?" She licked his bloodied lips. "'Cos I'll tup you fer free."

A fist of nausea crawled up Esme's throat. Staggering backward, she dropped her basket and clapped a gloved hand to her lips. She had to get away. Before she could hear what his answer would be.

Turning she bolted straight into Will's hard body, her fingers curling blindly in the heat of his shirt. "I'm sorry," she blurted, the world spinning around her.

Will's hand curled around her arm. "Steady there, Esme." His voice was surprisingly gentle. "I got you."

Bending low, he scooped up her basket and tucked her in close against his body. She needed it. Her knees were threatening to give out beneath her, a throb of white-hot anger searing away the hurt. The bastard. *Don't want no blood o' yours, Esme. I prefer it cold, out of the icebox.*

All this time she'd thought him afraid to take it fresh from the vein. They'd agreed–her and Blade–that it was best to let Rip sort himself out. He'd been so badly injured when he'd been infected... Without his own natural resilience, the craving virus had hit him hard and they'd virtually had to chain him in his room for the first month to stop him from tearing through the rookery after blood.

Esme had been patient. Six months ago, when Blade carried him in, blood dripping from his throat and abdomen...she'd thought she'd lost him. It didn't matter if she had to wait for him to learn control. She would. In her head, she'd always known that one day he would settle down

11

and then he would need to take a thrall to keep the craving at bay.

She'd had some insane notion that he might finally turn to her, after the last few years when he'd gone out of his way to keep a friendly distance.

And all this time, he'd been out getting blood on his own. Taking from... from whores on the street, when they wouldn't even know the basics of how to deal with him when he was in the throes of the hunger. The selfish, arrogant bastard. Not only was it dangerous but it was downright insulting. Her teeth ground together furiously.

"You all right?" Will asked, his voice sounding as though it came from a great distance away.

Esme straightened, her fingers locking around the basket he offered her. "I'm fine," she said tightly, slipping her hand into the crook of his arm. "Let's go."

Something hot trailed down her cheek, but at least Will was gentleman enough to pretend not to notice it.

CHAPTER 2

*R*ip shouldered through the back door into the enormous kitchen of the Warren.

A blanket of heat hit him, blood stinging in his cheeks and his heart racing. All he could see was the shocked look on Esme's face as she'd stood in the mouth of the alley, staring at him as if he'd just knifed her.

Hell. He hadn't meant her to see that. He knew exactly what she'd be thinking. She'd made it quite clear over the last month or two that if he wished to begin taking thralls, then she and Blade thought it best he start with someone who was experienced with a blue blood's volatile hungers. Her. Never mind that the mere thought of it set him on edge in a way any other woman would not have. Their friendship wouldn't have survived; if she knew precisely what he thought of her, she'd be horrified.

Esme looked up from the scarred workbench, those translucent green eyes locking on his then darting away. Will was seated on the other side of the bench, straddling a chair backwards with a mug of tea in his hands. Hot amber eyes lit on Rip in an eerie, not-quite-friendly way.

"Esme," Rip murmured. "You got a moment?"

Somehow he had to put this right. Explain to her that he'd never meant to take her as his thrall–that he didn't dare. She didn't owe them anything. She'd earned her right into this family over the years, no matter what the original deal of protection she'd made with Blade had been. Blade didn't require her services anymore and Rip was hardly about to make fresh demands on her. She was free of her thrall contract.

Esme scraped a pile of butchered parsley off the chopping board into a bubbling pot on the enormous stove. "I've got to get dinner on."

Rip shot Will a dark look and tipped his chin suggestively toward the door. "I'll help," he murmured. The way he usually did.

Will sat up a little straighter, setting the mug aside. His fingers curled around the back of the chair. Not going anywhere.

"That's quite all right. Will can help me." Esme put the chopping board down, a faint frown playing across her dark brows. Tendrils of black hair trailed down her nape as she stared down at the board for a fraction longer than necessary.

She wouldn't look at him. Rip's teeth ground together, the thought of Will's presence setting something off inside him, a flare of dark heat arrowing through his gut. Rip took a step toward her, hand curling into a fist.

"Esme, you weren't meant to see that–"

"Evidently." Setting a plucked chicken on the board, she picked up the cleaver and hefted its weight.

"I only meant–"

"You *said* you were fine." The cleaver cut into the board with a meaty thunk, separating the leg from a chicken's body.

"That you didn't require fresh blood. That you were drinking it cold, out of Blade's supplies in the cellars."

"I were," he snapped, staring down at the stiffness between her shoulder blades. *Look at me, damn you.*

The cleaver made another decisive move and Will winced as the impact echoed in the cavernous room. Slowly he levered himself to his feet. "Think I'll leave you two alone."

Esme's head jerked up. "What? Why?"

"Think you got matters to sort that ain't to do with me," Will replied.

"William Carver–"

Rip jerked his head. "Out."

Esme didn't like that none. She spun on him, her green eyes glittering with fury, the cleaver emphasising each word. "Don't you think you can order him out of my kitchen! I want him to stay. I want *you* to leave."

Will took his chance and bolted through the door.

"Looks like the decision's been made," Rip murmured softly.

As soon as he left, the room suddenly seemed too small. Rip scraped a hand over his mouth, feeling the rough scratch of his stubble. Esme looked down, her jaw clenching as she set about dismembering the chicken. If he wasn't mistaken he thought he heard a muttered, *"Coward,"* under her breath.

"I never meant you to be me thrall," he started to say, watching as the cleaver flashed up and then buried itself in the board. "Weren't ever me intention." He swallowed hard, remembering that first night when he'd put his mouth to her throat and drank. The flash of fire through his veins as though someone had injected him with pure acid, a rush of heat tightening in his groin until he felt like he was going to explode... And Esme... Helpless little gasping noises coming from her throat as she curled her hands into his shirt and begged, pleaded, for more. *"Yes... yes... Oh god, John!"*

15

If they'd been alone, if Blade hadn't been there... he'd have taken her. Shoved her down into his sheets and buried his heavy cock inside her, his teeth in her throat. The thought frightened him, because he didn't know where he would have stopped.

Or *if* he would have stopped.

Even now a clammy hand trailed down his spine. Safer to keep his distance, to satisfy his urges with a whore. All he wanted from them was blood. From Esme... he wanted everything.

"It's just blood," he said. "Don't mean nothin'."

"I *saw* you," she said, the cleaver hovering in the air. "I know exactly what it was. Do you think I don't know what happens between a blue blood and his thrall?"

That scored a blow. "Blade?" His voice roughened, though he knew he had no damned right to feel this way. Like he wanted to go after his master with a knife.

"Blade?" She laughed breathlessly. "It wasn't like that. Not between us. Of course I felt desire, but it wasn't—it was just my body's response to the chemical in his saliva. On some distant level I always knew that. And he never... never made demands."

Rip frowned, his hand easing over her wrist from behind. Curling around her grip on the cleaver. "Who then? You been with someone else?" he asked gruffly, enjoying the warmth from her body.

"Stupid," she whispered. "You are so stupid, Rip."

His thumb stroked hers, slipping the cleaver from her grasp. "What's this 'Rip' you keep callin' me?" She'd never called him that. Not in years. A little edge of panic curled through him. "You always called me John."

He liked the sound of his name on her lips. Too much so.

"So I did," she said in a toneless little voice that made the panic surge.

He put the cleaver down, his hard body curled around hers. *So small in his arms...* His gaze dropped to the curl that had come loose from her chignon and trailed against the smooth skin of her nape. Daring him to put his lips there. But why the hell would a woman as beautiful as she ever want his ugly hands on her? Rip steeled himself. "Esme, come now. We're friends. You always could tell me everythin.'"

"I used to think the same." Breaking free of his grip, she pushed past in a swirl of dark green skirts. "Before I realized you were lying to me." As he reached for her, she pulled away, hands held out of his grasp. "I've got to get this soup on."

Rip pressed a hand flat on the kitchen bench and stared at her. "Ain't stoppin' you. And what the 'ell you talkin' about? I don't know what's goin' on. You keep talkin' like this is over— like you ain't wantin' to be friends anymore." He stepped toward her but she backed away, a wary look on her face. Rip held up his hands incredulously. "I ain't goin' to 'urt you. You know that, aye?"

Wouldn't be the first time a woman backed away in fear, and it fucking hurt that she did. He'd never once lifted a hand, never once raised his voice... Growing up the way he did, out in the streets where he'd learned to be brutal, learned to use his size and speed to cultivate a reputation... It had protected him of course, when his mother couldn't. But it had also cost him.

Fear was just another weapon, but he hated the other flip of the coin. The isolation.

"Of course I know that."

Rip let out the breath he'd been holding. He didn't think he could handle it if she were afraid of him. "Then what the 'ell is this? I never lied. I said I were takin' me blood cold and I were. It's only been lately... Just three times. Weren't ever a lie, Esme. It just ain't seemed right to discuss it with you."

Scrubbing a hand over the roughened stubble on his head, he looked at her, trying to force her to see the truth. "Not the sort of thing I'd talk about with a lady, you understand?"

The look on her face made hope die in his chest.

"Esme?" he took another step toward her.

"I can't do this anymore," she whispered. "I have waited and waited… I just thought you needed some time."

"Can't do what?" His eyes narrowed, focusing on the part of the conversation that made his blood run cold. If he could just understand what the hell was going on in her head.

She gave a breathless laugh. "Friends, Rip. Friends. It doesn't matter. Forget I ever said anything." Running a hand through her hair, she stared at the pot on the stove with a blank look on her face. "Soup. I need to get the soup on."

He caught her arm as she hurried toward the stove and stared down at her. "Friends? You believe me? That I never meant to lie to you? You swear?"

Esme stared down at his hand. "I believe you." She gave a little tug. "After all, what in Heaven's name would you be trying to hide something from me for? Its not as if I have any hold over you."

He only wished the words didn't sound as sharp as they did.

THAT NIGHT RIP started knocking on doors.

None of the neighbours had seen anything at Liza Kent's and she hadn't mentioned that she would be away to anyone. The corner she usually worked was cold and empty and Rip stared at it for a long time before returning to her apartment. Nobody would notice her disappearance and if they did they wouldn't care. The corner would be claimed by someone else before too long and Liza Kent would vanish into the obscurity of just another Whitechapel disappearance. *Like his mother had.*

The body of Flash Jacky was exactly where they'd left it. Usually Blade had men who handled the clean up, but Rip was loathe to involve him. And if he were honest with himself, he needed this. Bending low, he tugged aside the gaping slash in Flash Jacky's shirt and examined the wound. Looked like a knife but then he were no expert on wounds. Only on dealing them.

Luckily he knew someone who was.

Pounding on the door to Doctor Creavey's, he held his breath for the stink that was starting to creep through the blanket he'd wrapped around Flash Jacky. Heavy footsteps sounded on the other side of the door and then Creavey peered out at him through his half-moon spectacles, his eyes narrowing on the body Rip had thrown over his shoulder. His red-rimmed eyes were watery and his thin wiry hair stuck out in grey tufts. There was more of it in his mutton chops than on the top of his head.

"Two pounds," Creavey snapped.

Rip simply stared at him.

Creavey cursed. "Its after hours, Rip. Man's got to make his living."

"After 'ours?" Rip asked, shouldering over the stoop. "Or were you and your lads just gettin' set to 'ead out."

Creavey blanched. "What do you mean?"

"Wouldn't do to 'ave some of me boys come around diggin'," Rip said deliberately, knowing full well what the disgraced doctor paid some of the local grave-robbers for. Creavey's obsession with death was so far harmless; as long as it stayed that way Blade intended to leave him alone. He had his uses.

Creavey paled. "I suppose I can spare you a few minutes. Through here, if you will."

The small set of rooms Creavey let were above a shop. They consisted of two separate rooms for his bedchambers and a small sitting room, connected to his surgery by a long, glass-roofed hallway that served as his laboratory. Chemical permeated the air. Rip took a sniff but it wasn't quite the same smell as had been used at Liza Kent's. That had seemed to burn in his nostrils and obliterate any chance of smelling anything else for hours–this was a combination that reminded him of the dizzying rush when they'd taken the mangled remains of his arm off after the accident and grafted the steel socket straight into his shoulder joint. Creavey's rooms always made him feel uneasy, his head spinning. Best to get this over with quickly.

He strode through into the laboratory and dumped Flash Jacky on the long bench that lined the wall. Pots and burners slid out of the way, a variety of metal implements scattered on every possible inch of bench. A dead rat was pinned to the timber, its intestines spread as if in delicate curiosity. Rip's lip curled.

"Not there," Creavey sighed in exasperation. "The surgery."

With a grunt Rip hauled the body up and followed Creavey into the small room. Two sheets were draped over a pair of still forms on the steel examination tables. Creavey directed him toward the last table and then dragged his stained apron off its hook. It strained over his rounded belly.

Rip stared at one of the other bodies beneath the sheet, smelling the stale hint of graveside dirt and rot. "What 'ave you got 'ere?"

"Arsenic poisoning," Creavey replied in a distracted voice. "A long, slow case of it, by the look of the white lines on his fingernails and his thinning hair. The wife, I suspect. Barely any mystery at all. So what have you bought me?" Creavey tugged a pair of goggles over his head.

"You tell me," Rip replied, crossing his arms over his chest and leaning back against the doorjamb. The smell was stronger here, reminding him somewhat of what had been dropped at Liza Kent's place. "What's that smell?" he asked.

"Formaldehyde," Creavey replied, gesturing toward the shelves.

Little jars covered them, filled with tiny deformed bodies. That was how Creavey made most of his living; absolving ladies of certain inconveniences. The hair's on Rip's arm rose and he shifted, dragging his gaze away. It weren't natural but Creavey paid good money for them.

He paced the far end of the room, tempted to scrub at the tiny erect hairs on his arm. An unnaturally pale hand hung out from under the far examination table, a puckered red line across the wrist. Not difficult to guess what the cause of death there was. Rip turned around, unnerved by how white the woman's skin was. Drained by her own hand.

Hanging a lantern high against a mirrored backdrop that reflected the light down onto the body, Creavey cut the blanket off Flash Jacky and leaned closer. Dragging the amplifying goggles down over his eyes, he peered through them, using a pair of long metal forceps to tug the scraps of fabric out of the way. "Hmm."

Creavey measured the length of the cut. "This was an upward slash," he muttered. "Left handed, by the look of the angle." Leaning closer, he hooked the tip of his forceps inside the ragged top edge of the wound and peered inside. "Jaysus."

"What is it?" Rip asked, striding closer.

The good doctor had paled; whatever it was, it had to be dire. "I'm not sure yet… Here, hand me that scalpel."

Rip paced the concrete floor near the drain as the doctor sliced Flash Jacky open from throat to pelvis. Using shears and a saw, he cut through the rib cage until Rip had to turn away and stare at the wall.

"Here," Creavey called and pointed. "The weapon came up beneath the sternum–an upwards thrust through here... But it also came out here. Like the blade was curved..."

Rip frowned. "A hook?"

"A razor-sharp hook," Creavey said, stepping back and wiping the gore from his fingers. Some of the colour had drained from his florid face. "The type found down on the wharves and commonly used by fisherman, and also–"

"Slashers," Rip finished, staring at Flash Jacky's grisly remains. "The bleedin' Slashers."

"I would have to complete my findings but I believe this is the cause of death." Creavey tugged at his apron strings. "I thought Blade done for the Slasher gangs six months back?"

"'e did," Rip replied, though a vampire had actually taken care of that. Its haunt had been in Undertown, the dark world that had once been the ELU underground line before half the tunnels collapsed. Only the poor or the very desperate lived there–or the Slasher gangs that had once run rampant through this part of the East End. Initiation into one of the gangs required the sacrifice of a limb, preferably by your own hand. Every single one of them had been enhanced with a metal hook or knife, the blade grafted into the forearm in rudimentary rookery style. Some even had wheels for feet or beady glass eyes that didn't quite focus on the world properly.

Slashers stole people from their beds and dragged them down below, where they drained a body of its blood to sell to the Echelon's draining factories. The type of scum Rip didn't mind running afoul of–preferably with his own knife.

"It's the way of the East End," Rip explained gruffly. "Take out one of the groups in power and others spring up like mushrooms." He thought of Liza Kent's flat, with its very obvious symbol carved into the door. No slasher could have missed it and being on the edges of Blade's turf it was clear what this was. "Whoever they are, they're challengin' Blade. Taken one o' 'is."

"Someone with no interest in continued existence," Creavey muttered.

"Aye." Rip stepped back. This explained the disappearance of Liza Kent. Poor girl. No doubt her withered carcass would surface in the streets, drained of all its blood. "You ain't seen a thing o' this, you understand?"

Creavey wasn't a foolish man. "I'll bury the body myself. Make sure nobody but me sees it."

Rip glared at him. "Just you make sure you bury it. I don't 'old with none of this cuttin' dead bodies up, you 'ear me?"

"Getting hard to find bodies, Rip."

Rip stared at him. Hard.

"How else is a man to know the secrets of death?" Creavey protested. "You don't know how much good this could do."

Rip took a step back, ready to leave the stench of death behind him. "One day someone's goin' to show you a first'and look at it, if you keep this up. Just you think on that."

CHAPTER 3

*D*awn silvered the sky. Esme tossed in her narrow bed then finally gave a sigh and threw the covers back. No point lying here. All she'd do was start thinking about Rip and that was the sort of thing that had kept her up half the night.

No sense crying over spilt milk, her mama's voice whispered in her ear.

Easy to say. Not so easy to do.

Dragging on her heavy wool robe, Esme hopped across the chilly floors and sank her feet into her luxurious slippers. All the way from the Orient, Blade had assured her when he gave them to her. Horribly impractical, but then every woman deserved to have something frivolous.

Her breath misting in the air, Esme hurried out into the hallway and down toward the kitchens. She needed to stoke the coals in the enormous hearth so there would be hot water to wash with.

The routine was soothing. This was the time of day she liked best, when the world was hushed and quiet and she was completely alone. After taking a bucket of warm water upstairs and swiftly performing her ablutions, she returned below, her hair tucked up neatly and her midnight-blue skirts swishing around her ankles. Above her she could hear people starting to stir, the peace of the day threatening to shatter. Though she loved the odd little family Blade had collected over the years, right now she simply wished to be left alone.

Grabbing her shawl and basket, Esme pushed out into the cold Winter's morning and stopped, her breath catching at the glittering array in front of her. The whole world was white, the drift of snowflakes floating slowly through the air. Esme's breath steamed and the biting cold caught in her lungs but even that was a thing of beauty. The air tasted so pure, so clean, as if the snow had dampened down even the thick pall of smog that clung to London's steeples.

Her boots crunched in the soft, powdery snow as she wrapped her shawl around her, tucking it tight. It had been years since it had snowed like this. A clump slid off a nearby roof and Esme jerked her head up. The silence suddenly took on an ominous sensation, all the little hairs on the back of her neck lifting.

Nothing moved. Still... the sensation of being watched heightened. Tugging her gloves on slowly, she stared out into the street. This was ridiculous. Everybody in the 'Chapel knew she belonged to Blade. Nobody would dare lay a finger on her.

Gathering her breath, she strode out into the narrow lane... and directly into a warm, hard surface.

Hands locked around her upper arms as she staggered back, the scent of heated male curling through her nostrils. Panic flared as she instantly recognized whom it was. She'd washed his shirts for years; she'd recognise that distinct, slightly spicy scent of his cologne anywhere.

"Rip," she blurted. "What are you doing out?"

25

"Ain't been in," Rip muttered, staring down at her with an unreadable expression in his green eyes. "So it still ain't 'John'?"

She ignored him, breaking free of his hold and patting a strand of hair into place. It was petty, but he'd hurt her yesterday and part of her wanted him to feel some damned disappointment too. "You'll be looking for your bed then," she said, sidestepping him and tucking her basket in tightly against her abdomen. "If you'll excuse me? I have errands to run."

The soft shuffle of his heavier footsteps echoed hers and she ground her teeth together, suddenly furious. Why wouldn't he leave her alone?

"There's hot water in the cistern by the stove. You'll be wanting a wash, I believe," she threw back over her shoulder.

Two long steps and he caught up to her, his hands shoved deep into his pockets and his collar pulled high against the drift of snowflakes. Canny green eyes raked her. Rip had never been a fool, though most people took him for one.

"Know when a woman's tryin' to give me the 'eave-'o, Esme." He stared straight ahead. "I'd ask why, but I think it's got ought to do with what 'appened yesterday."

Silence was a sudden, awkward wall between them.

"I was trying to be considerate," she replied stiffly. "You'll be tired."

"Stop tellin' me what I feel and what I ought to be wantin'," he snapped. "You know you can tell me anythin', don't you?"

"Of course."

When she said nothing else, his lips thinned. The soft dawn light softened the harsh slant of his brow and the jagged break in his nose, but he would never be handsome. Still... For a moment, her heart twisted in her chest as she stared at his familiar profile. So strong. So stubborn. She'd stared at that face for years, wondering what thoughts he entertained behind those fathomless green eyes.

Jerking her eyes away, she focused on the street. Theirs were the only footsteps marring the pristine white. It made her feel terribly alone with him, her body prickling with dangerous awareness. And that only made her furious with herself.

"You're angry with me," he said gruffly.

"I shouldn't think why." Esme strode ahead, desperately wanting to avoid this conversation.

A steely hand caught her upper arm and when she spun, he was staring down at her with those far-too-clever eyes. "We can dance in circles all day, Esme, but the 'onest truth is I ain't got a bloody clue why you're so upset." He rubbed his forehead, fingertips leaving white marks in his swarthy skin. Frustration gleamed in his eyes. "I spent 'alf the night thinkin' 'bout it."

"Let me go," she said quietly.

"No."

"Damn you, J—Rip! Get your hands off me!" She threw all of her weight against his grip and felt his hand slip on the fabric of her sleeves.

He held them up in surrender and she staggered back. The thin rigid spars of his left hand reflected the morning light. As if sensing where her gaze was drawn he jerked it low, shoving it in his pocket, a flush of heat turning his cheeks ruddy. "So I'm thinkin' right, 'bout what you said yesterday, and I'm thinkin' this 'as got nothin' to do with me so-called lie."

Esme swallowed. "I see."

Those wicked eyes narrowed at her non-committal answer. "You're angry with me," he said slowly. "Because I were drinkin' me blood from someone else? Because you thought you'd be me thrall? I should 'ave told you I wouldn't

'old you accountable to that. You don't need to be me thrall–
you don't need to be anyone's thrall."

Esme shook her head, trying to step around him. How to
tell him she'd wanted to be his so desperately? Especially
when he'd made it clear he didn't think of her in that way. A
flush of heat burned behind her eyes. "It doesn't matter–"

He grabbed her again. "Damn it, Esme. I'm tryin' to work
this out." Hard fingers–metal and flesh–dug into her upper
arms as he stared down at her. "I'm tryin'. Please. Tell me
what's wrong?"

"What's wrong?" Suddenly she couldn't hold it in any
longer. It was either this or burst into tears. She shoved past.
"I—I have my pride, John Doolan. I do! I won't beg you,
damn it. You don't want me and I won't–"

He danced in front of her and Esme staggered into him,
hands pushing at his chest.

"I don't want you?" he demanded. "I don't want your
blood?" A dark glint came into his eyes. "That's it, ain't it?
That's what this is 'bout? Because I don't want your *bloody
blood*?"

Something hot slid down her cheek and she dashed the
tear away, hoping he wouldn't see it. "Leave me alone," she
said hoarsely.

The wall of his chest stiffened. "Esme?" he said. "Are you
cryin'?"

"N-no."

Suddenly his hand cupped her jaw, the cool iron of his
right one slick against her skin. Esme shut her eyes as he
tilted her face up to his, one last tear sliding silently down
her cheek. She didn't want him to see it but the firm grip
gave her no choice.

A roughened thumb traced the tear's path. *"Fuckin' hell,"*
he said in a breathless, bewildered tone. "Christ, luv. Don't
cry. Please don't cry. I ain't worth that."

"Yes, you are," she blubbered, swiping angrily at his arm. An old argument. "I won't have you belittle yourself." Everyone else did enough of that.

Ugly as sin, the whores on the street whispered. Oh yes, she'd heard it and knew he had too. But in her heart, sin wasn't unattractive at all. It was the faint brush of his hard body against hers as they passed in the kitchen or the slow, dangerous smile he gave her when they were alone and he was stealing batter from her cake mix. Only she got to see what no one else did when he dropped his guard and let himself be just a man, instead of forcing his reputation and his scowling menace down people's throats.

"Fine, luv. Fine. Won't say it."

His hard body surrounded her, fingertips caressing her jaw so lightly she could have escaped if she'd wanted to.

He still didn't understand what the problem was. A part of her wanted to laugh bitterly but she knew why he simply couldn't fathom her interest. She could walk away now, knowing that their friendship would remain as it always had, that her nights would be spent in a torture of thwarted desire whilst he lay on the other side of the wall, no doubt oblivious to her true feelings.

She could pull away. She should.

If she wanted to...

Her fingers loosened from their tight fist and flexed wide, hovering above his abdomen. Esme couldn't believe what she was suddenly thinking. She was so damned tired of waiting for him to notice her feelings. Of being too afraid to voice them.

"Do you want to know why I'm so upset?" Esme whispered, forcing the words through trembling lips. If she couldn't say this now, then she never would.

"Aye," he said gruffly, tilting his face lower as if to find the answers in her eyes.

"Because I *wanted* it to be me," she whispered, sinking her fist into the collar of his shirt and lifting onto her toes to press her lips to his.

RIP FROZE, sucking in a sharp hiss of air between his parted lips.

He could taste her on his mouth, in the warmth of her breath... Everything he'd ever dreamed of and couldn't believe was actually happening.

Esme's soft body wilted into his, her fists curling in his shirt and her mouth closing over his with a hungry little moan. The dart of her tongue lashed through him, as though it flickered directly over the length of his cock. He was hard in seconds, his hands sliding into the coarse stiffness of her bustle as he wrenched her against him.

Esme.

Christ. Rip hesitated, a furore of emotion swirling through him. *Dangerous.* The heady drumbeat of her pulse was suddenly thick in his ears. She dragged his head down and captured his mouth with a wantonness that showed she knew exactly what she wanted. Rip staggered forward, taking her with him. Somehow her back hit the wall and then he was pressing against her, hand fisting in her skirts and need burning through him like a raging river.

A flash of red swept behind his closed lids and Rip groaned, his hips thrusting unconsciously against her. *Steady.* He forced his fingers to unclench in her skirts but Esme bit his lip, a flare of pain and pleasure shooting through him.

Her breath. Ragged in his ears. The taste of her, burning through him, igniting every desire Rip had. Her pulse. Her god-damned pulse, thundering now. Rip groaned, wrenching his mouth from hers. Esme's hand curled in his collar as if she wasn't prepared to let him go but he had to get away. If he didn't he'd be on her, teeth digging into the smooth column of her throat, his hand dropping to the blade at his waist... Another groan as the thought fired his blood.

Get away. Now.

Rip shoved back and staggered into the streets, blinking against the dark shadows of his vision. Movement screamed around him. The predator in him, the hunger, was so furiously aware of Esme, of the throb of her heart, that he didn't dare take a step toward her.

"John," she whispered, touching her lips. Her eyes were almost glassy.

Esme took a step forward but he backed away, shoving his hands into his pockets. *Christ.* Couldn't she bloody see how close to the edge he was?

He shook his head abruptly. "Don't."

Esme froze.

"I'm sorry," he said. "I can't. Not with you." The look on her face almost crushed him. As if he had hit her. "Gotta go. I just... I can't."

Then he turned and stalked through the steady drift of snow toward the Warren, listening to the sharp, hurt intake of her breath as he tried to stop himself from bleeding her dry.

CHAPTER 4

*T*he bristling fir tree went up, the tip bending against the ceiling. Will peered through the branches, his arms wrapped around the evergreen and a scowl on his face as he wrestled it into place.

"Isn't she a beauty?" Blade asked, stepping back and examining it.

Esme pasted a smile on her face and nodded as the rest of the men gathered to look. She could feel Rip watching her from the other side of the tree, leaning against the wall in silence. He'd barely been involved in wrestling the tree inside and neither had she. Both of them hovering on the edges of the family, as if someone had trapped the pair of them outside one of those snow globes the French exported, looking on the family within. Somehow the world seemed dulled, sound distorted. As if she didn't truly belong in this moment.

Honoria laughed as Blade slung his arm around her. Since marrying Blade, she'd put on several pounds, a vital improvement. The weight softened her features and happiness often put a smile on her face. In the past six months she and Esme had become quite close, though Esme couldn't go to her with this. She couldn't go to anyone, not even Blade, who'd once been her confidante. Her heart felt like it was breaking but how could she tell her friends what had happened?

She'd kissed Rip and he'd told her he didn't want her. *I can't. Not with you.* Words that seemed scarred across her heart. She felt it bubbling up inside her, like a fist in her throat, threatening to escape. But if she let it, the tears wouldn't stop. And Esme had always been good at hiding them.

She hadn't cried when her parents cut her off after marrying Tom and she hadn't cried when his mother cast her into the streets after his death. Instead she'd picked herself up out of the gutters and found herself respectable employment as a seamstress until her new neighbour began to make life unbearable. She could do it again. Paste a smile on her lips as she pretended that nothing had ever happened between she and Rip.

Still, the thought of being his friend right now was more than she could bear.

Two children darted past, screaming with laughter. Lark had arrived at the Warren with Tin Man, though nobody knew whether she was his daughter, a relation or merely some young girl he'd taken in off the streets, and Charlie was Honoria's younger brother. Though he'd been stricken with the craving too, he'd recovered from it much quicker than Rip had. Blade kept an eye on the lad, but he seemed to be handling himself well. In the first few months he'd been terrified to be alone with anyone human, especially his sisters Honoria and Lena, for fear of going for their throats. It was good to hear his laughter now and see him relax.

"Charlie! Give it back!" Lena darted into the room, her hair tied up in a red ribbon and her cheeks flushed. She stopped when she saw the tree, her eyes widening. On the verge of being a woman, Lena could still be given to moments of childish glee. And her life had been hard enough six months ago that she'd took to every moment as if it could be the last.

"Goodness," she said. "Where did that come from?" Then her eyes narrowed in delight as she spotted Will, straining to hold the tree in place. "What a terribly hairy decoration. Perhaps we should put some ribbons on it?"

Will shoved out of the branches as if embarrassed to be caught up in it. He'd stiffened as soon as Lena entered the room.

The sight jolted Esme out of her misery. Will had never liked women much, ever since his mother sold him to a travelling showman and he'd spent ten years in a cage. It had taken Esme years to break through his distrustful demeanour—mostly by sneaking him snippets of roast beef and baking spice cakes for him. Stepping up to his side, Esme slid a protective hand over his shoulder. "I think it will hold," she said.

Their eyes met. Will's shoulders softened, as though relieved to see her. Esme wasn't stupid. She'd seen him duck behind buildings to avoid Lena, whilst Lena mercilessly hunted him down. Lena knew she made him uneasy, but she hadn't quite realized why.

It was difficult enough for Will to trust Esme and Honoria but a young, attractive girl who flirted with him? Esme had never seen him with a woman, but she knew when a young man desired a girl. And when he didn't quite know how to deal with it.

"Come help me in the kitchen," she said.

Rip watched them go, his arms folded across his chest and his green eyes locking on her with an intensity that unnerved her. He shifted as if about to follow them, then thought better of it.

Good.

Her cheeks burning, Esme ducked past Blade–ignoring the inquisitive look he gave her–and pushed through into the kitchen.

A wall of heat hit her. Comforting, homely... her own special retreat. She'd spent the last hour popping corn whilst the men dragged the tree inside and fluffy mounds of it filled a bowl on the bench to be strung up for decorations for the tree. Little mince pies still warm from the oven flavoured the room with their meaty scent and Will's amber eyes locked on them.

"Here," Esme murmured.

The tenseness leeched out of him as he sat and began devouring mince pies. Esme reached out with a smile and brushed the hair out his eyes. She'd never had a brother, but Will was as close as one could be.

"You shouldn't let her get to you," she murmured.

Instantly he stiffened.

"And before you tell me a lie, please bear in mind that I'm the only one who has noticed."

Will's eyelashes fluttered against his cheeks as he swallowed his mouthful. "Ain't nothin'," he finally said, dusting the crumbs of pastry from his fingers. "Lena's just a girl, playin' games she can't afford to. I don't intend to do aught about it, though I should, just to teach her a lesson."

"You might be the one who gets your fingers burned," she replied. "Honoria's protective of her sister and therefore so is Blade."

Frustration flared in his eyes. A verwulfen's temper was always volatile and Esme prayed that Lena would learn that before Will did something he didn't want to do. He'd always been so fiercely controlled, knowing the devastation he could cause if he lost himself to the berserker fury. A verwulfen wasn't like a blue blood, hungering for blood, but the rage was almost as dangerous as a blue blood's hunger.

"I try to stay clear o' her," he murmured, hints of Scotland in his words. "It's hard when she lives here too. Been thinkin'... maybe its time I found a place o' me own, aye?"

"Perhaps you should find a woman."

At that he shook his head abruptly. "No. That ain't for me."

"Have you ever been with a woman?" she asked softly, knowing the answer. Though Blade had only spoken of it once, she knew there'd been that moment between them, when Will turned eighteen and first became Blade's thrall. She could only imagine how confusing it must have been for Will, for the feeding affected him at least as much as it did her.

Somehow Blade had sorted the misunderstanding but Will was still wary enough of most women that he rarely tolerated them. The only one he'd ever shown any hint of attraction to was in the next room and blithely unaware of the confusion she was wreaking.

"Christ, Esme." Will's eyes flared wild. "I ain't talkin' about this with you."

"You should speak to someone," she chided. "Perhaps Blade?"

"He'd strip the skin off me back if he knew what I were thinkin'," Will admitted gruffly.

"John?" she suggested.

A quirk of one tawny brow. "'Cause he obviously knows what he's doin'."

"What do you mean by that?" She stilled.

Will reached out and slid his hand over hers on the bench. "Don't like to see you hurtin'."

That hot rush of pain swam through her. Esme

summoned a brave smile. "I'm fine, Will. I just don't believe I can be a friend to John at the moment. Not… Not just yet."

Movement flickered at the corner of her vision. The door swinging shut. Esme's head jerked up and she stared as Rip's eyes met hers. Heat flushed into her cheeks as his gaze slid over her hand, so secure under Will's. He had to have heard her. For a moment her mind raced, trying to remember if anything else had been said.

Rip's gaze dropped to the floor. "Blade wants your 'elp with the tree," he said to Will. "Lena wants to put an angel on the top."

Will stood with fluid grace, sighing under his breath. "She would."

As he left the room, Esme toyed with her apron strings. "I didn't mean–"

"I 'eard you," he replied softly. "Per'aps… Per'aps it's for the best."

With a bleak nod in her direction, he turned on his heel and disappeared.

CHAPTER 5

*R*ip prowled the night, his body on edge almost as much as his nerves. Running a hand over the stubble on his scalp, he stared out across the frost-rimed rooftops. Scars rippled beneath his fingertips; the reason he razored his hair so short. If he grew it, thick silvery half moons gleamed in the coarse blackness of his hair and Rip preferred not to look a fool.

His fingertips traced the deeper scar at the base of his spine in a familiar rhythm that helped him think. A half circle. Shaped like the bottom of a bottle. Or, more accurately, a broken bottle. The scar's jagged edges bore testimony to that.

No matter how much he tried to keep his mind on the business at hand–he had the midnight guard shift–he couldn't stop thinking of Esme. *Jaysus. What in blazes was he going to do?* She'd kissed him on the mouth, her body pressing against his as if she were almost greedy for him. At the time he'd been so afraid he'd hurt her that the shock of it hadn't begun to set in.

But he'd had all day to think, his mind chasing itself around in circles. What had she meant by it?

"Because I wanted it to be me…"

Seven little whispered words that tore his chest in two. What had she meant by it? Did she mean that she wanted to be his thrall? She'd never once given him any indication that their friendship was anything more–had she? Only that first night, when he'd taken her blood and she'd gasped as her fingernails dug into his back. But that could have been the feel of it. A feeding could take a woman–or man–like that sometimes.

And now she wanted nothing to do with him.

The worst thing was, he didn't know how to fix it. Oh, she smiled at him and spoke to him, but he felt as though there were a wall between them. Treating him with polite courtesy until he choked on it.

Shadows flickered in the distance, melting beneath the moonlight. Rip froze, peering across the stark snow-blanketed rooftops. Too big to be a cat. Whatever it was they were gone now but the uneasy feeling remained.

Footprints left their mark behind him as he crossed the rooftops that served as his own private highway here in the rookeries. The streets were as crooked as an old man's grin and cramped with refuse and the odd shivering human. But up here the world was clean and he could seemingly see for miles.

He knew as soon as he hit Angel Alley what he was about to find. Blood was thick in the air, a metallic scent in the freezing night. Footsteps mingled on the roof, leading directly to the edge of the wall that circled Whitechapel to keep the Echelon out. South. Toward the nearest entrance to Undertown.

"Hell," he swore, trying to breathe through his mouth.

Saliva pooled. Go after the Slashers? Or check to see if there was anyone alive down there?

A soft whimper made his decision for him. So quiet that no normal human would hear it. Quiet as a mouse.

Swinging over the edge of the roof, he saw the window in the attic and dropped to the ledge, the muscles in his forearm bulging. Easy work to break the latch. He'd cut his teeth as a cracksman. Of course, it had been easier when his shoulders weren't as broad.

Moving quietly, Rip eased through the narrow window, landing with cat-like silence on his toes and fingertips. The smell of blood was stronger here; a god-damned aphrodisiac. His head spun, the hunger clutching at his guts with iron claws. Another scared, panting gasp came from below and he tracked the sound, the faint whisper of breathing and the barely-stifled sobs.

More blood. Still warm. He just had to find the source of it...

Swallowing hard, Rip ground his head into the palms of his hands. Not his thoughts but the demon within. Damn it. When would this ease? When would he stop seeing everyone around him as merely a source of nourishment?

Or would he?

He'd seen the blackness rise in Blade's eyes many times. Was that what he had to look forward to?

"*Mama?*" A little voice whispered, down in the dark.

For an instant all the years rushed away and that was him. Locked in the cellar and listening to the sounds of fists pounding on flesh. His mother's muffled gasps as she tried to spare him the worst of it.

The hunger was thick and unquenched in his throat but suddenly Rip found he could breathe through it. Looking up, he sucked in a lungful of air and scraped his hand over his face. *Come on, you ugly brute*, he snarled to himself. *Or do you want to let the Slashers get away?*

And that was enough to choke down the last desperate grip of it. Fury rose. Nothing he hated more than Slashers.

With cold purpose burning in his chest, he straightened himself to his full height and started down the stairs. Halfway down they creaked and the stifled sobs froze. Not even a breath now.

He could smell the blood, splashes of red darkening his vision. Rip took each step precisely, looking around at the small kitchen. Two rooms branched off it. A veritable manor here in Whitechapel.

"I ain't goin' to 'urt you," he called. The silence had a listening feel to it. "I'm one o' Blade's men."

Nothing. Only a ragged heartbeat thumping wildly in the dark. He pinpointed its location–beneath the floorboards– and stepped slowly toward it. The rug in the middle of the floor was skewed. A man lay on the bare timber near it, his blank eyes staring at nothing. No doubt he'd bought his child's life with his death.

The remains of a meal rested on the table, cold herring pie congealing on the tin plates. The knife and fork at the head of the table were placed beside the plate in an orderly manner, the chair tucked back in. The other two seats were scraped back from the table, one fork lying forlornly on the floor.

Rip examined the room. One of the paintings near the door hung skewed. A fight then. He bent low, examining the man's body and trying not to breathe too deeply as he pieced together what had happened. Someone had knocked at the door. The man got up to open it, and judging by his bruised knuckles, realized what was standing there as soon as he had it open. He fought, which gave the other two enough time to shove away from the table. Maybe for the mother to hide her child in the small trapdoor beneath the rug.

The woman's screaming absence told the story. Rip's gut dropped like lead. Another one missing. But why hadn't they taken the child?

Panicked breathing sounded beneath his feet. Rip dragged the rug back and spread it over the man's body. There was no sign of a lock on the square-cut trapdoor. Which meant it was locked from the inside.

Perhaps they'd seen him out there on the rooftops, or didn't want to waste the time trying to rip at the trapdoor?

Or perhaps they'd gotten what they wanted. He was starting to remember who'd lived here now, a nice young couple with a tow-headed daughter. Oliver Tanner and his wife... He couldn't remember her name. But he'd seen the daughter before. Meggie? Maggie? No, definitely Meggie. Peeking out from behind her father's leg when he came to pay his tithe to Blade for the cost of protection.

Sure as rain, there would be a pair of crossed daggers over the lintel.

Another message. Another taunt.

We can take any you claim to protect.

Rip sank onto the floor beside the trapdoor. "Meggie?" he called softly, trying to lower his voice as much as possible. "Meggie, I need you to open the door. I'm 'ere to 'elp you."

Another shuddery sob.

"Won't 'urt you," he said. "I'll take you back to Blade's place, where you'll be safe. Can't naught get at you there." Silence. "Please, Meggie. Open the door."

He could tear it apart. He had the strength now. But he knew what it was like to hide in the dark, knowing that your only safety lay in the thin bit of wood from a cupboard door. He wouldn't take that away from her. He wouldn't add more nightmares to those she undoubtedly had.

"Meggie, I can't find your mother," he called. "I need to get you away from 'ere so I can go look for 'er. You want that, don't you? You want me to try and find 'er?"

"They took her–" A choked voice blurted. "I could 'ear 'er screamin'."

Rip listened to her frightened sob. "I'm gonna go after 'em, sweet'eart. I just need you to let me in."

Silence. Then a lock snicked.

Rip let out the breath he'd been holding. "Okay, luv. I'm goin' to open 'er up. Don't be frightened." He wet his lips. Her fear was a heady thing. "I know I look mean, but I'm only mean to them as deserves it."

Slowly he tugged the iron ring from the floor, lifting the edge of the trapdoor. The light gleamed on the wet-shine of a pair of frightened eyes. Slowly he reached down and offered her his left hand. The flesh one. Right now, if she saw the cold metal of his mech-hand she might think him a Slasher. He'd had that before.

A minute ticked by. Rip stayed still, letting her make her own judgements. Finally Meggie reached up and wrapped her small fingers in his own. As he dragged her out, she looked around but Rip caught her face and pressed it to his shoulder. Moonlight gleamed through the window, just enough to highlight the splashes of blood on the floor and the body beneath the rug.

She didn't need to see that.

"'ush, luv," he whispered, stroking her hair as she cried into his shoulder. It was the most he could spare her, after burying his own mother at the age of eleven.

Meggie had descended into a sightless misery, sobbing against his shoulder as if she couldn't hear anything he said.

Rip wrapped her in a blanket and took her to the one person he knew might be able to help.

The Warren was quiet this time of night. Rip knocked on Esme's door, feeling the little girl cling to him tighter, as if afraid he was going to let her go. The instant trust left him feeling slightly uncomfortable—and infinitely tender.

Footsteps crossed the floor and Esme opened the door, her dark hair in a loose plait and a robe dragged over her nightgown. As soon as she saw him that cool veneer swept over her features, then she saw the little girl in his arms.

"Oh," she murmured, hands coming up to stroke Meggie's hair. "What happened?"

Slashers, he mouthed.

Esme's eyes softened in distress. "Here now, sweetheart," she murmured, stroking the red curls out of the girl's face. "What's your name?"

"Meggie," he replied, looking down at the warm weight. "Meggie, this 'ere's Esme. She'll look after you whilst I–"

Meggie's grip tightened. "No. Don't leave me!"

Rip's hand paused on her hair. "I need to find your mother. I've got to go, sweet'eart. Esme will keep you safe." He stroked the fine red curls. "You 'ave to let go, darlin'. The quicker I can get goin', the more chance I got o' findin' 'er."

He wouldn't give her false promises.

He'd give her this however. "And then I'll make certain those men don't ever get another chance o' doin' this. I'll make 'em pay, just for you."

He could feel Esme's gaze on him, watching. "You don't mind?" he asked. The coolness of her own manners rubbed him raw.

"Of course not," she replied, reaching out.

Rip turned and offloaded the child into Esme's arms. She was good with children. Of course, it helped that she always smelled faintly of baking biscuits, cinnamon and spices. If anyone could look after the frightened little girl, it would be her.

The warm scent of her skin drifted past his nostrils as her arms brushed against him. Taking Meggie, Esme buried her face in her red hair and hummed under her breath. "It's all right, little one. If anyone can find your mother it will be John." Soothing the hair out of the little girl's face. "Even the slashers are afraid of him."

A hint of pride in the words. Rip stared at her, wondering if she even knew how much her voice had softened. His fingers jerked, wanting to reach out and touch her, to ask what was so bloody unforgivable. No point though. She'd flinch away no doubt. No. His rough hands weren't for her.

"Got to get goin'," he said.

Green eyes met his. "Of course." As the silence stretched out between them, Esme's lips parted but the words never came.

"Righto," he muttered, taking a step back from her. With a sharp nod, he turned around and shoved his hands into his pockets, feeling his chest tighten with despair. *Hell.*

"Rip!"

Rip paused and glanced over his shoulder.

"Be careful," she called, though he sensed that wasn't all that she'd intended to say. "You watch your back tonight. You know what the slashers are like. I don't want to have to... to be washing the blood out of your shirt in the morning."

With a gruff nod he started down the hallway. Time to wake Blade. This was no longer something for one man to deal with.

CHAPTER 6

"*Y*ou ought 'ave told me sooner."

The same words he'd heard Blade repeat for the last hour.

Rip's jaw tightened as he bent low and heaved the sewer grate out of the cobbles, his biceps straining. "Thought I could 'andle it."

Blade put both hands on either side of the open grate and dropped his body through. Leaning the grate covering against the wall, Rip knelt and followed him. Darkness swallowed him whole as he landed with a splash.

Undertown was a rabbit warren of tunnels and boarded up rooms carved into the world below the East End. Once an attempt to push the underground train lines into the East, the scheme had collapsed with the tunnels. Nearly two hundred workers had died in the shadowy depths, trapped beneath rubble or buried alive in the small niches of tunnel still open.

Rumour said the tunnels were haunted, but that didn't stop the poor or the homeless from moving in. Or the Slasher gangs.

However this sewer was empty of everything but rats. They skittered in the dark, their frantic hearts beating loudly in the stillness as Rip sloshed along in Blade's wake.

Blade paused at an intersection, faint light streaming through from a grate above. Shadowy bands crossed his closed eyes as he scented the air. "This way," he said, turning with unerring focus to the left. "I can smell the blood."

The stench of the sewers killed any hints of blood that Rip could smell, but then, Blade had nearly fifty years of being a blue blood. And his virus count was much higher; dangerously high in fact. As such, his senses were almost as refined as Will's.

"Let me go first," Rip said, pushing past. Old habits died hard and he'd been too long Blade's bodyguard not to be cautious.

As he followed the tunnel, he finally caught a hint of copper. Blood. They'd tracked the trail from Meggie's house. Someone—most likely Meggie's mother, Annie—was bleeding. Not heavily though. He could almost imagine the odd drop of crimson splashing into the murky water, diluting instantly.

At least she'd still be alive. She had to be. The Slashers needed her blood flowing through her veins to extract it properly. Blue bloods refused to drink what they called 'stale blood'. Or deadman's drink, in the vernacular.

"Wanted to ask you what's goin' on with Esme," Blade said suddenly.

Rip's shoulders tensed and he paused, glancing back over his shoulder. "What do you mean?"

Blade sloshed past, as if his words hadn't thrown the cat amongst the pigeons. "She's been off-colour lately. Thought you might 'ave some idea as to why, seein' how close you two been. Why?" Blade glanced back. "You two 'ad a fight?"

Rip wasn't fooled by his master's relaxed stance. The

green of Blade's eyes glittered in the near-dark. The one thing he took extremely seriously was the health and happiness of those he considered under his protection.

Still... if there was one person who might know what the hell was going on, it was Blade. Rip's experience of women was limited to brief assignations in the dark. He let out a rough sigh and followed. "Don't know," he admitted. "She ain't 'appy with me at the moment." The kiss suddenly sprang to mind and he was glad Blade wouldn't see the hot flush that swept his cheeks.

"You said somethin'?" Deceptively casual.

"Nothin' I know of." A pause. Then, "She got it in 'er 'ead I meant 'er to be me thrall. I tried to set 'er straight but she took it wrong."

"You don't want that?"

"Christ," Rip swore. "No. I don't know—We're friends. Don't want nothin' comin' between that." He swallowed hard. "You know what it's like, the 'unger. Don't want to scare 'er, to 'urt 'er." Another curse under his breath. "It ain't just the blood lust. Don't want Esme thinkin' I expect more. Thinkin' she 'as to give me 'er flesh rights."

"What if she wants to be your thrall?"

He laughed under his breath, an incredulous sound. "Aye. Just what every woman dreams of."

"You undervalue yourself."

"No. I don't. I know what people see when they look at me." He'd encouraged it.

"Course they do. That's the problem with forgin' a reputation in our line o' work. Don't know you, do they?" Blade asked. "But Esme does. Don't insult 'er by stickin' 'er with that bunch o' fools."

Rip splashed along, the leather of his boots damp and miserable. *Her lips pressed against his...* Why had she kissed him? Could Blade be right?

"She said anythin'?" he asked suddenly. "To you?"

"Ain't 'ad much time to get 'er alone lately," Blade replied. "Can see she's upset though. You two actin' like a pair o' strange dogs thrown in a room together."

"We'll work it out." He hoped.

"Aye." Blade paused, cocking his head to listen. "'Ear that?"

Rip stilled.

Eerie laughter suddenly echoed through the tunnels. Rip's hand found the familiar leather hilt of his hunting knife as he waded to Blade's side. "They know we're 'ere?"

"Aye." Blade's expression tightened. "Let's go greet 'em."

There was a hole in the wall of the sewers, rubble spilling into the water. An iron ladder led into the darkness below. Rip peered through. Could be anything waiting. As Blade moved, he caught his arm.

"Let me go first."

"Expect anythin'," Blade said with a curt nod.

Rip stepped through into the opening. The ladder vanished down what looked like an old air vent. Below he could see fan blades slowly circling. Bending his knees, he leapt out into the darkness, air whipping past him as he dropped.

Landing in the middle of the fan, he knelt low to absorb the shock, his eyes adjusting to the dim light that streamed from the open vent above. The fan blades had once been dull but now sharp edges gleamed as they circled below him. Rust coloured stains edged them.

Another crude opening had been hacked into the wall. This was a part of Undertown he'd never explored. Close to where the original underground train tunnel had collapsed.

"Careful," he called.

Blade landed beside him, the tails of his leather coat slapping his thighs. Rip steadied him and nodded at the hole in the wall.

"Looks like someone missed." Blade noticed the bloodstains.

"Unless they were thrown," Rip replied. He shouldered through the small tunnel.

Just big enough for him. It left him at a disadvantage for he could barely swing his arm, let alone a knife. By the time he reached the end he'd have been sweating if a blue blood could.

Light beckoned ahead. The narrow tunnel opened into an enormous cavern of shadows. From the slight breeze, it must have gone a fair ways. As his eyes adjusted, Rip saw the platform stretching into the distance.

One of the abandoned stations that had once been carved beneath London. No doubt the tunnel he'd just come through had been hacked out by someone of an enterprising nature, trying to unearth their own little hidey-hole in the caved-in sections.

Movement shifted. Rip stiffened as a man stepped out of the darkness, dragging a young woman in a stained grey gown. Dusty red curls tumbled over her dirt-marred forehead and her eyes were glazed with pain and horror as the man sank a hand into her hair and yanked her throat back.

"Come on out, little rats. I see you," the man called, taking a sniff of the stale air. "I smell you."

Tall enough to fill out the brown coat he wore. Rip examined him ruthlessly. Whoever he was, this man knew how to fight—and dirty. The fingertips had been cut from his gloves, but razor blades gleamed over his last knuckles, where'd he'd cut them through the leather. Land a punch with them and they'd tear a man to shreds.

A cap covered his hair, his cheeks gaunt and dirty, though the way he stood—as if he were King of this lair and they supplicants—gave Rip some idea of his character.

Behind him, slashers crept out of the shadows, crawling

low on hands and knees as they fanned out. Armed with an assortment of knives and bludgeons, they bared teeth and snarled in Rip's direction.

"You afraid o' Bloody Bill 'iggins?" the leader called. "You 'eard o' 'im, ain't you? 'Eard what he can do–"

Rip stepped forward, sliding his hands into his pockets. "Can't say rightly that I 'ave," he called. "Slashers come. Slashers go." A shrug. "They all bleed the same colour in the end."

Higgins's smile died. "You'll know me fuckin' name by the end o' this. I'll carve it in your bloody forehead."

Behind him, Rip could hear Blade fanning out in the other direction.

"All this," Blade called, "to get me attention? Should 'ave just left your callin' card. I mighta gotten round to you. In the end."

A knife came up, pressing against Annie's throat. Higgins dragged her back against his chest, hissing through his teeth as she gasped. "That were me callin' card. Thought you'd like the blood."

Rip stilled, shooting Blade a look. The man was on edge. Mock him too much and he'd cut her throat just to taunt them.

"So what d'you want?" he called. "Why the games?"

"I want the 'Chapel."

Blade laughed. "She'd eat you alive, boy-o."

The knife cut just enough to break Annie's skin. "Please," she whispered.

"Let 'er go," Rip called, taking a step closer. "She got no part in this."

Higgins pressed his lips to her cheek, never taking his eyes off the pair of them. "She's the bait. The good times. The fun." Shutting his eyes for a second, he rubbed his cheek against hers, as if smelling her. A long trickle of blood slid down the muscle of her throat and pooled in her collarbone. Bill licked it. "You ever drained a lass? They fight it at first. Kickin' and screamin'... Then you see 'em startin' to get sleepy as the blood drips." Looking up, he smiled. "You cravers think you own the world, but you're afraid o it, afraid o' the power. You could drain the world dry and they'd not be able to say nay, but you don't. Keepin' your thralls alive. Takin' sips when you ought to tear a lass's god-damned throat open." A mad light came into his eyes. "I'd make a better blue blood than all o' you."

"You want to be a blue blood?" Rip snarled. "Then come and get me blood."

"Nah. Want you to put your weapons on the ground and kick 'em over. Slow like. Then I'll take what I want."

Rip didn't even look to see what his master was doing. He held up the two hunting knives strapped to his thighs and dropped them, listening to the metallic ping. A pair of brass knuckles followed, then the longer knife he wore sheathed down his spine.

Kicking them over, he waited as Blade did the same.

All they needed to do was wait for the moment Higgins let Annie go. She was all that stayed his hand.

His gaze slid to her throat and the slow drip of blood there. Rip fought the urge to swallow. Whispers of darkness blurred his vision for a moment. *Hunger.*

Think of Meggie. Think of bringing her mother home to her.

"That's the way." Higgins smiled and gestured to his men.

They crawled forward and snatched the assortment of weapons. Blade was still stripping knives out of his boots and leather waistcoat. Near on a half dozen of them.

Fools. Neither he nor Blade needed a knife to be dangerous.

"Turn around," Higgins said.

"Let 'er go," Rip replied.

"Let 'er go?" the bastard laughed. "Aye, I'll let her go…"

He jerked the knife hard, slashing across the inner skin of her wrist. Annie screamed as blood splashed over her grey skirts. Tumbling away, she cupped a hand over the wound, blood dripping between her fingers.

Rip took a step forward then stiffened as six slashers stepped in front of Higgins.

"Take 'em down," Blade said softly. "I'll 'elp the girl."

This. This he could do. Rip stepped forward, letting the red haze, the anger, the fury wash over him. For a second Annie's frightened scream sounded like his mother's that last time.

"I'm goin' to kill you," he whispered, fists clenching.

One of the slashers darted forward, swinging a chain with lethal dexterity. It whipped toward him and Rip dodged, his hand lashing out and catching the end of it. Chain links wrapped around his fist and he yanked hard, bringing his other fist through as the slasher stumbled off-balance toward him.

The heavy crunch of his fist in the man's throat was distinctly satisfying. The slasher went down with a gurgle and Rip stepped over him, swinging the other end of the chain up into his mech hand and tugging the links taut. Three of them leapt for him, knives flashing in the dim light. Rip didn't think. Leaping forward, he wrapped the chain around one of their throats and yanked the ends over each other hard enough to break the neck.

A hook slashed toward his face, breaking his hold. The body he held went down, still twitching and Rip swung, blocking another blow. Grabbing the slasher's forearm he snapped his open hand down into the man's elbow so it bent and shoved the hook back toward the man.

Screaming, the slasher went down with his own hook stuck in his eye. Rip bent low as the next man leapt for him and threw him over his shoulder.

Each move was like a dance, the men coming at him as if they moved through a waltz. That was one of the benefits of the craving; increased speed. The demon within howled for release but he held it, forcing it to glut its hunger on pain and not blood.

Within seconds the six slashers were down. Only the one with the hook was still alive.

Higgins's nostrils flared and he gestured the other four in front of him. "Kill 'im," he snarled, stepping back into the beckoning shadows of the train tunnel. A hunchback lingered there, holding a small shuttered lantern; the source of the light.

This time Rip smiled. His vision was nothing but a shadowscape, in tones of blacks and greys. Men came at him and he cut them down with little more than his bare hands.

His reputation might keep most in the 'Chapel from fixing to mess with him, but he'd earned it in blood and pain over the years.

Behind him he heard Blade whispering to Annie. The blood roared through his veins, red rushing through his eyes. Seeing Higgins step off the platform onto the train tracks made the hunger roar. Rip lifted the last slasher over his head and hurled him after the bastard.

"Coward!" he snapped, striding forward. Dropping onto the tracks he stepped over the slasher he'd just thrown. "You want to frighten little girls? You want to abduct women who can't lift a 'and to you–" And there was his mother's face again, wide-eyed and pleading as she lifted her arms up to protect her head.

Mama, no!

And Whitey, bringing the bottle down for the last time. The last fucking time ever–

Fury roared through him. Higgins shoved the hunchback toward him and Rip barely paused to throw him aside.

"You come and fight, you fuckin' coward. You fight me, fight a man."

Higgins stepped back into the mouth of the tunnel. Silver glinted at the sides but Rip was too enraged to care.

"I think not," Higgins said. He took a step back, then another, eyes glittering in a watchful way.

Rip stepped toward the mouth of the tunnel—

"Don't move!" Blade snapped.

Only years of responding to that tone made his body freeze. A flicker of disappointment flashed through Higgins's eyes then he shrugged and took another step back. "Another time, p'raps." Dragging a small metal box out of his pocket, he pressed the button in the middle of it.

With a groan, one of the silver blades on the side of the tunnel dropped, swinging past his nose by an inch. Rip leapt back as others released from the sides of the tunnel, whooshing past with deadly force. Like the swinging pendulum on a grandfather clock, each blade moved independently of the others so that all he could see were flashes of Higgins, slowly stepping back through them.

An entire bloody gauntlet of them.

"Been makin' a few adjustments to me new home," Higgins called. Doffing his hat, he stepped back, slashes of him appearing between each swinging blade. "Tick, tock, gentlemen." Then with a laugh he disappeared into the darkness.

"Damn it!" Rip kicked the side of the tunnel and shot a frustrated look toward his master. "I damned well 'ad 'im."

"Aye, 'e knew it too," Blade murmured, staring through narrowed eyes after Higgins. "Them's the sort as always runs when the ship starts sinkin'. Like bleedin' rats."

Blade knelt down, gathering Annie into his arms. He looked up, black eyes gleaming. The blood from her wrists dripped all over her gown and she gave a weak whimper. Rip realized he was staring.

"I got 'er," Blade said, lifting her wrist to his mouth and licking the wound. "Get on after 'im. I'll send Will to 'elp you and meet you back at the Warren when you both done."

Rip's breath caught. He couldn't look away from the blood.

Blade's eyes narrowed as he put his mouth to the woman's wrist and suckled. "Go," he snapped. "Bring me back his bleedin' 'ead."

Rip nodded sharply, jerking around and facing the swinging pendulums. Blade could do what he couldn't; use his saliva to heal the broken skin, hopefully before she lost too much blood. Rip would never have been able to control himself in such a way.

Each scythe swung in a random pattern, leaving bare inches between them. Not enough for his body to rest between each blade. He'd need to time this perfectly...

Taking a deep breath he stepped forward, feeling a cool breeze over his face as the first scythe swung past. Another step, an odd dancing movement, again, and again. Focusing sharply on each blade until he was finally at the end of the gauntlet. Breathing hard, he stared into the darkness. The same vinegary tang he'd smelt in Flash Jacky's cancelled out all other scents. A beaker of chemical to obliterate any trace of Higgins.

Couldn't track him by scent then.

Well, that was fine with him. He'd spent thirty-five years without enhanced senses. He knew this world, of darkness and grime. And he wasn't afraid of the dark. Not anymore.

Indeed, the dark should fear him.

CHAPTER 7

*N*ight was falling.

Esme looked up from the stove as her ears caught the faintest hint of noise. Swallowing hard, she put her wooden spoon down on the bench and hurried to the door to peer out. The yard was empty. No sign of Rip. Blade had returned hours ago with Meggie's mother, Annie, and a murderous look on his face. He'd snapped an order at Will to get out and help Rip search for the slashers, then he'd bellowed for Honoria to get her medicine kit together and vanished into his rooms with the two women.

After spending most of the afternoon in Esme's lap, Meggie had recently gone up with Lena to sit with her mother as she recovered. There was no point in Esme being there as well. Her skills lay in another area and she sought her own comfort in baking tonight as the shadows lengthened and Rip still hadn't returned.

Latching the door, she sighed under her breath and returned to the stove. The fresh scent of cinnamon buns steamed in the air and Esme stared through them. She'd always worried about Rip when he was out on patrol, but it had been worse ever since the vampire attacked him. Before that he'd seemed so large, so full of life that it seemed as though nothing should beset him.

When Blade brought him home, covered in blood and still trying not to drown on all the fluid in his lungs, she'd been nearly undone. She'd buried one husband–she didn't wish to bury another man that she cared for. Once was enough.

It didn't matter if things were strained between them. Didn't matter if he saw her as nothing more than a friend.

A sharp rap at the door made her gasp. Looking up, she saw Will peering through the glass, and behind him the thick leather jerkin that she knew belonged to Rip.

"Oh, thank goodness," she said, opening the door to the pair of them. Her gaze darted past Will, raking over Rip's large body. He was covered in blood, one sleeve of his shirt torn.

"Blood ain't his," Will assured her, stepping past.

"Did you find them?" Esme asked, unable to take his reassurance at face value. But indeed, the blood looked more like spatters, not as though it dripped from him anywhere.

"Nothin'." Rip wore a scowl fierce enough to make grown men quake. As he stepped past her, he paused, looking down. Their eyes met and Esme's breath caught on all the things she suddenly wanted to blurt. She couldn't stop herself from reaching out, touching him, just to make sure he was truly there. The backs of her fingers brushed his chest and Rip sucked in a sharp breath, a hint of red burnishing his cheekbones. He looked up and she followed his gaze to where Will arched a brow.

Then she smelt him. The scent was ripe enough to make her nose wrinkle.

The spell was broken.

"Aye," he muttered. "I stink. Goin' up to wash. Sorry 'bout the blood. I'll throw the shirt out so you don't got to wash it."

And with that he shouldered past, leaving her alone with Will.

Esme's mouth worked but nothing came out. Drat the man. She'd spent the past three hours wearing a rut in the floor with worry and he could barely speak to her. A bite of guilt edged down her spine. Her own fault. She was the one who'd decreed they couldn't be friends, at least until she'd recovered from the pain of unrequited feelings.

But what kind of friend did that make her?

Will shrugged. "He were upset we couldn't track the man. They dropped some sort o' chemical again, obliterated all scent. Let him be. He's in a dark mood tonight."

Esme nodded, staring at the staircase Rip had ascended. She'd never had it in her to be cold for long and even now guilt stirred her to run after him.

The hurt gleaming in his eyes... The sense of failure she'd seen there. He'd take this upon himself, for that was the type of man he was.

Perhaps she could put aside her hurt feelings and simply try to be a friend?

Esme took a deep breath. Instinct told her to let him go, but that was cowardice more than anything. "There's stew in the oven if you're hungry," she said, patting Will's arm. "I have something to do."

The look in his eyes told her he wasn't fooled. Esme untied her apron and tossed it on the table, then hurried after Rip.

Esme knew where she'd find him. Blade had his own private wash-chambers, but the rest of them made do with a communal bathhouse. The water was piped in from the boiler-pack behind the kitchens, sinfully hot, and the tub was large enough for two.

She could hear the taps running as she paused by the door, her breath catching with last minute nervousness. No point running now though. He'd have heard her soft breath.

Esme rapped sharply, before she could convince herself otherwise, and waited.

"Aye?" Rip called, water stirring as he sat up.

"Are you decent?" she asked.

There was a long moment of silence. "I'm in the bath," he replied.

Decent enough. They didn't sit on formalities here in the Warren. Esme took a deep breath and pushed inside.

Rip sank down with a splash and a yelp, the water sloshing over his waist and stomach. "Christ, Esme. What the 'ell are you doin?" A look of something raw and almost violent crossed his face, and he slammed his hands over his groin.

"There's nothing I haven't seen before," she reminded him, closing the door behind her. "I am a widow, John."

"Aye, well ain't a man entitled to his privacy?" he snarled.

The first hint of anger she'd heard in his voice. Esme examined him. Not anger. No. She'd never seen him so discomposed before. Rip was nothing if not confident.

But then she'd never seen him stripped before. She knew he didn't like to display the gaunt steel of his mech arm, as if he'd had one too many turn from him in fright. Here in the East End a mech limb meant you were either a slasher, or one of the mechs that ought to be bound in the enclaves to work off their mech-debt. Either way it was a sign that you weren't quite human, or not human enough for some.

She didn't linger long on his arm though. The rest of him caught her eye. Oh, she might have imagined what he'd look like beneath those heavy, oilskin coats he wore, but the reality... the reality was breath-taking.

All sleek, heavy-set muscle, slightly flushed from the heat

of the bath. Golden skin that gleamed beneath the lantern-light. He'd razored his hair and beard again, so that the hair was barely stubble. Thick and black, it gave him a villainous look, but he was her villain.

"I thought you might need a friend," she replied, crossing slowly to the bath.

Rip watched her warily, water streaming over his curled up knee from the faucet. He shifted, as if to cover himself better. "Now you want to be friends? Christ, Esme. I don't understand what's goin' on wit' you." His voice dropped. "And you could 'ave better timin'. This ain't... it ain't decent."

The flush of heat through his cheekbones made her smile, despite her hurt. "I never suspected you'd be so prim."

Those wicked green eyes met hers. "'Ow 'bout you strip off and I'll get dressed and we'll see how composed you are?"

"There's enough soap in the bath to keep you decent."

He looked down, bubbles licking at his mid-riff. Still, he didn't draw his hands away. "Still ain't right."

"I wasn't aware you'd read Lady Hammersley's Rules of Etiquette." Despite herself, she couldn't help teasing him. "Besides, you've had your mouth on my throat, John. That's rather more intimate than this, wouldn't you agree?"

He looked away, not to be drawn by her teasing. A part of her deflated. "Why are you 'ere?"

Esme paused by the stand that held the bath oils and soaps. Picking up a vial of rosewood oil, she sniffed it, then stoppered it again. Blade was always one for signs of decadence. The wash-chamber could have been found in one of the Echelon's homes.

"I thought you might want to talk," she said quietly. "You looked upset when you came in through the door."

Water splashed as he reached for the faucet and turned it off. Esme watched him hungrily, smelling the next scented oil. Too lemony.

"Ain't upset. Just… frustrated." He leaned back in the tub, legs drawn up to fit his length. Bubbles clung to the thick dark hairs on his muscular thighs. "I thought I could 'andle this by meself. Didn't tell Blade 'til tonight."

"You knew the slashers were in the 'Chapel?" She looked up from another vial sharply, surprised that Blade wasn't angrier. He took his duties as master of Whitechapel seriously.

"Thought I could 'andle it," Rip repeated with a growl.

"Did Blade say anything?"

"Aye." A gruff warning for her to drop the subject.

Esme idly sniffed another vial. Sandalwood. She'd always liked the smell. Grabbing a bar of soap and a wash cloth, she took the oil and crossed to the bath.

Rip didn't quite stiffen but she could sense the tension in his body. Another jolt to the heart. His disapproval of this was clear.

"Relax," she murmured, feeling it sharply in her chest. Hurt brewed up, but she pushed it aside. Tonight wasn't about her.

Sitting on the lip of the bath, she dunked the washcloth into the water. Rip almost leapt out of the bath. "Christ. What are you doin'?" he asked suspiciously.

Esme soaped up the cloth. "Washing your back," she replied, wishing he didn't sound as if she'd suggested he roll in a dead cat. "You can't reach."

Steeling herself, she put a hand to his shoulder and pushed him forward. Rip complied, wrapping his arms around his knees stiffly.

If she'd thought his arm muscly, then she had never quite glimpsed his back. The bulk of his trapezium and neck were as thick as one of his thighs. Esme rubbed the washcloth gently across his shoulder, leaving a trail of lather behind.

She'd done this for her husband once and the thought

made her miss him, just for a moment. Tom had been a good man. So different from Rip. A merchant's son who liked to read and knew so much that it amazed her. Still, he'd had his flaws. He couldn't see that his mother despised her–Ellen would have hated any woman he married. And he'd been short-sighted enough that he hadn't foreseen how Esme might survive after he died of consumption. He'd told her time and time again that his mother would see her well off.

Eight long years she'd been alone. It hadn't bothered her at first. She'd loved Tom and the grief of losing him had been all she could think of at first. But as grief softened, she'd started to become aware of all the things she missed; a man's touch, his smell, the feeling of joy when she spent all afternoon baking for him.

Esme slowly soaped Rip's back, sliding the cloth up over his shoulder and down his chest. She had to rest her hand on his other shoulder to reach, her fingertips touching cool metal. The edges of his skin were ragged and puckered where the steel met it. Rip quivered as if his skin were highly sensitive there.

"Blade said you killed some of the slashers," she murmured, caressing the heavy slab of his pectorals.

"Not enough."

"You shouldn't be so hard on yourself. Every one of them that you kill means one less to harm the innocent."

"Slasher gangs spring up like mushrooms," he muttered. "Can't get rid of 'em. Always those 'ard enough to see no other way to live. Coin's a good lure."

"You brought Meggie's mother home," she reminded him.

Rip sighed. "It were Blade. I couldn't—couldn't go near 'er. Not with all the blood."

"Aye, well, Meggie thinks you're a hero. You were the one who promised her you'd try and find her mother."

"Ain't no 'ero."

"You are to me," she whispered. "You saved a frightened little girl and her mother."

Their eyes met and Rip said nothing. Still, she thought he looked pleased with her words. Or accepting, at least.

Slowly he relaxed back against the bath, tipping his head back against the lip of the tub. The muscles in his throat worked as he swallowed, his dark lashes fluttering closed against his cheeks.

Esme continued her slow, hypnotic movements, unable to take her eye from his face. Sinking the cloth below the water, she dragged it up, dripping water across his soapy chest. Rip shifted, his eyes fluttering open as she delved beneath the water again, but he soon settled once he realized the movement was innocent.

"This is nice," he admitted.

"I used to do this for Tom," she mused. "Or sometimes I would climb in with him."

Stillness. "You miss your 'usband."

"Of course I do." She clenched the cloth in her hands, wringing it out. "It was a long time ago though. Another world." And she preferred the rough edges of the Warren, with its warmth and cheers compared to living with Tom and his mother, no matter how much she'd loved him. A guilty thought, but true.

Rip seemed to think on that. "Surprised you never married again." He looked up at her as she dropped the cloth on the stand and picked up the vial of sandalwood oil.

"Perhaps nobody has asked me," she replied, with careful neutrality.

"That butcher on Abbott's Lane took a liking to you." His words seemed just as careful.

"Lots of men have 'taken a liking' to me in the last few years. And not one of them plucked up the courage to do anything more, with Blade's sign of protection tattooed on my wrist." She let the oil drip into her cupped palm and then set it aside, rubbing her hands together. "Lean forward."

Rip eyed her hands. "What are you doin' now?"

"Have you ever seen me knead dough?" she asked as he sat up again. Sliding closer, she settled directly behind him.

"Aye."

Esme reached and slid her hand over his shoulders and neck, the slick-shine of the oil gleaming on his skin. She was generous with it, rubbing her palms over his shoulders and down his chest, then dragging them back up his arm. Rip shifted, but the stiffness had leeched out of him again.

The feel of his skin was like rough silk beneath her palms. His chest was hairless, his nipples tightening as she flickered her fingers over them. Another little tease and one that made his breath catch. Not quite immune to her then.

Just not interested.

She buried the pain and concentrated on stroking the smooth muscles of his neck. To please him. And, if she were honest with herself, to please her. She liked touching him, however innocently. She'd like to touch him not so innocently too. To dip her hand beneath the water and wrap her strong fingers around his cock.

Rip relaxed into her touch as Esme's thumb slid over a hard knot above his shoulder blade. She dug her fingers in, earning a grunt and gently worked it. Running her knuckles up his neck and down again.

"You've got strong hands," he murmured. Another gentle groan as he leaned back against her. "God, that feels good."

"Mmm." Too good. Stolen moments. Stolen touches. Still, he seemed to enjoy having her hands on him almost as much as she did. Esme eased her touch, rubbing her thumbs up under where his scalp met his neck.

Rip groaned as her fingers dug into his scalp, feeling the soft prickle of his hair. His head fell back against her thigh, eyes closed in utter bliss as she kneaded his scalp with her fingers.

He didn't seem to realize that the oil was dissolving the bubbles on the water's surface. They vanished with alacrity until oil gleamed on the surface, hinting at what lurked beneath the surface. Esme was no virgin. She looked and the sight thrilled her.

He was not unaffected. Not at all.

Leaning down, she pressed her lips to his forehead, her fingers stilling and her heart thundering in her chest.

Rip blinked sleepily. "Thank you," he murmured. "You didn't 'ave to do that."

"I like looking after you," she replied, staring down into those very-green eyes. So close. All she had to do was lean forward and press her lips to his...

"You do too much," he muttered. "You ought to let us take care of you sometimes."

"I'm the housekeeper," she reminded him.

"This ain't part of your job."

Esme paused, idly circling his temples with her fingers. "Perhaps I like looking after you."

He looked up, green eyes serious. "You ought 'ave married again, Esme. You were made to 'ave a husband. Some man to... to give you babies. Make you 'appy."

The words took her by surprise. Hurt flared again and she sat up straight, thoughts of kissing him fleeing from her mind. How easily he spoke of her marrying someone else. As if the thought wouldn't bother him at all. If he had mentioned another woman she'd have been sick with jealousy.

It only served to prove precisely how he saw her. A friend. Not a lover. Not a... a potential wife. Or consort. No doubt the stirring of his body was simply a man's reaction to having a woman touch him. Not because he desired her in particular.

Coldness trailed over her skin. A dull, hollow feeling in the pit of her stomach. Reality was flooding over her. She had hoped that he might feel something more for her. But he didn't. Friends. Always friends.

"You're right," she found herself murmuring. "I should have married again."

Instead she'd waited for him. Lost the last few years hoping and waiting. Her time was running out. Rip was right. She did want children. Desperately. And now she was almost five-and-thirty and her years of child-bearing slowly narrowing ahead of her.

But the thought of taking another man to bed made her feel sick. Whenever she'd dreamed of babies, they'd had green eyes and black hair. His eyes.

Esme slowly stood, her shoulders sinking. The brutal realization that he didn't want her–that he'd never want her–washed over her like ice water and she couldn't help a shiver. "I'll leave you to get dressed," she murmured.

Then she turned and hurriedly left the room.

RIP SLIPPED OUTSIDE, the cold air stinging his cheeks as he cupped his hands and lit a cheroot. If he cocked his head, he could hear the quiet murmur of Esme's voice as she showed Meggie, Lark and Charlie how to string popped corn and holly berries on thread for the tree. Though her voice was soft enough to lull the children to sleep, it set him on edge tonight.

He didn't understand her. Barely able to speak to him all day, then coming in–whilst he was naked–and easing him with soft words and gentle hands. Touching him as if she cared, then blithely announcing that he was right–perhaps she should have married again.

He couldn't deal with this. The hunger itched under his skin, Esme confusing him. A man'd almost think her presence in the washroom a proposition.

Don't be an idiot.

She'd made it quite clear it wasn't.

Rip crushed the cheroot under his heel and tugged his coat tight, burying his hand in its warm folds as he leaned against the shadowed arch of the doorway. The cold was almost biting, but it helped to clear his head. Somehow he had to put this right. Make sure he understood what was going on in her mind. Blade had only muddied the waters, suggesting that perhaps there was more to it than Rip suspected. Making him hope there was more.

Rip needed to talk to her, but with everyone underfoot, managing to get her alone was a lesson in frustration. Esme wasn't making it any easier. Avoiding him again. *Christ.*

The door to the kitchen opened, heat and laughter spilling out. Rip froze, sinking deeper into the shadows as the very object of his confusion stepped out into the yard, her boots crunching on the snow and her hands tucked up under her armpits. Her thick black hair was knotted at her nape, the dark wings of her brows drawn into an intense frown. Those translucent green eyes were distant however. Blind to the world around her.

Witchy eyes. The first time they'd met his she'd put a spell on him, like a punch to the chest.

Now was his chance. Rip rocked onto the balls of his feet then froze as another pair of boots crunched into the slush. Blade shut the kitchen door behind him, the rectangle of light Esme stood in vanishing. With his enhanced vision however, Rip could see them perfectly.

And hear them.

Blade had to know he was there. His own senses were superb, unless he was particularly distracted. Rip barely dared breathe.

"What's wrong?" Blade asked.

"Nothing," Esme replied.

Rip eased back into the shadows of the overhang as silence settled over the yard. After a moment Blade sighed. "Course it ain't. Don't think I'm a fool, Esme. Or blind. Any 'alf-wit could see you're upset and people is startin' to ask why."

The angry swish of her skirts. "What have you told them?"

"Same as you've told me. Nothin'."

More silence. Rip pressed his back into the bricks, straining to watch and hear.

"'ave you told 'im?" Blade muttered. "Bout 'ow you bin feelin'? Because I could—"

"Don't you dare say a word to him," Esme gasped. "You promised you wouldn't. Let me deal with this."

Rip frowned.

"Runnin' away ain't dealin' with it, Es."

"I'm not running away." Esme's shoulders slumped, a look of pain flickering over her face. "John doesn't want me."

Rip froze. Him. They were talking about him.

A slash of light from the kitchen window cut across Blade's face and his tawny eyebrows arched. "'E don't want you? 'E told you that?" Even from this distance the words were incredulous.

"He said he couldn't... Not with me." The words were a choked whisper. "The other day I kissed him and he shoved me away as though... as though—" Her face screwed up. "And tonight...He virtually told me I should have married someone else."

"Aw, 'ell." Blade stepped forward and dragged her into his

arms as she started crying. "Don't cry, luv." He looked up suddenly, light gleaming off his green eyes as they cut directly into the shadows where Rip was watching. "Sure there's got to be a reason for it. Man'd be a fool not to see what's right beneath 'is nose."

Rip's blood seemed to slow through his veins. The sight of her crying was like a knife to the chest... but he couldn't have moved toward her if he tried.

Esme wanted *him? Not as a friend or a master, but as a lover?* The world seemed to skew on its axis, words and conversations between them taking on new meaning. *Why the hell hadn't she told him?*

"He doesn't want my blood," she sobbed. "He told me he never had any intention of taking me as a thrall."

"Thought you wanted more'n to be his thrall?" Blade asked.

"I do... I did..." she faltered. "I'm not a young girl anymore, Blade. I've buried a husband and forced myself back to my feet after his mother threw me into the streets." Head lowering, she whispered, "I forgot what it was to hope, to dream. I should have known better. Dreams don't exist. Not here."

Blade sighed and kissed her hair with rough affection as she drew her face away from his shoulder and rubbed the wetness from her cheeks. "Don't lose that, Esme. Of all o' us, I ought be the one who knows what it's like to lose 'ope, but I found it again." He gave her one last squeeze. "You'll sort matters with Rip. But you tell 'im from me that he ought to treat you right. Do the right thing by you." His voice lowered in warning. "Or else."

And that was for him.

Esme scraped the last of the tears from her face. "There's nothing to sort out," she said sadly. "I can't do it anymore,

Blade. I can't." Her voice dropped to a whisper. "There's no point in dreaming of something I can't have."

Blade stilled, staring down at her. "Give it some time, luv. Things might change now 'e's got an inklin' o' your mind."

Esme drew back and wiped her eyes, exhaustion bruising her fine features. "I shouldn't see why. He made his intentions clear."

"Funny thing... intentions. Maybe 'e didn't understand yours?" Blade drew back. "You comin' inside?"

She shook her head, dark hair gleaming. "Not yet. I don't want anybody to see I've been crying."

Blade stared at her for a long moment. Finally he nodded. "I'll see you in the mornin' then. Just... Don't 'ate me, luv."

"Hate you for what?" Esme frowned in confusion.

Blade took several steps back, toward the door. "Interferin'."

"How did you–" She froze then and Rip knew that she'd realized they weren't alone. Shoulders stiffening, she turned with a horrified look on her face, eyes darting through the shadows of the yard as she searched for him.

Blade took the chance to disappear into the house. *Coward.* Rip's fists flexed as Esme looked for him, the metal one creaking as the joints tightened.

Esme's head tilted toward him as if she heard it, her breath catching.

"John?" she whispered.

No chance to fade away as he dealt with the sudden confusion that left him almost breathless. Rip stepped out of the shadows, sliding his hands into his pockets. Instantly her eyes lit on him and they stared at each other across the yard, the silence thick and heavy. He couldn't breathe, all of a sudden. She looked so beautiful, even with the track of tears down her face. And frightened and confused.

He didn't know what to say.

Esme's gaze darted toward the door as if in betrayal. Slowly she looked back at him, her shoulders stiffening with hurt pride. "How long have you been standing there?"

"Before you come out," he replied quietly.

Her chin quivered. "You heard it all?"

He nodded.

"Mercy," she whispered, taking an unconscious step toward the kitchen.

Rip leaped forward and grabbed her arm. "Don't," he said roughly, the pad of his thumb stroking the soft wool of her sleeve. "You and I need to talk."

Esme's swollen eyes dropped to his hand but she was too exhausted to fight him. Without looking at him, she nodded. "Where?" A whisper.

Rip looked across the yard at the old stables Blade used as a storehouse. "This way," he murmured, his hand sliding into hers as he dragged her toward it.

BLADE SWUNG through the kitchen door with a platter of mince pies and a fist clenched around the neck of a bottle of blud-wein. He looked entirely too pleased with himself. Honoria took the platter from him and passed it to Lena with a swift instruction to offer them around.

"What are you up to?" she murmured, as her husband rested his hip on the edge of an armchair and tugged the cork free of the thick green glass with a wet *plonk*.

Blade winked at her, his smile warming her all the way through. She never grew tired of that smile. "Meddlin'," he said, sliding an arm around her waist and tugging her against his body as he set the wine aside.

Honoria looped her arms around his neck. "Where's Esme?" She realized who else was notably missing. "And Rip?

What have you done? You told her you wouldn't say anything to him."

"Didn't." Blade's grin widened further. "That don't mean I ain't allowed to let 'er say as much as she wants when I know 'e's listenin'."

"You didn't!"

Blade dragged her closer. "Consider it me little present to Esme. She'll thank me once it's done."

"She won't be thanking you now."

"True." Blade grinned and kissed her lips. "Now, why don't you take me upstairs and give me *my* present."

Honoria gave in. The man was a devil and he knew it. "I didn't buy you a single thing," she declared.

"That's all right," he purred. "We'll think o' somethin'."

CHAPTER 8

*L*ight flickered to life as Rip struck a lucifer and crouched low, sliding the match into the lantern so the wick caught. The shadows lengthened and danced back as he focused with frightful intensity on the flame, the acrid scent of phosphorus in the air.

Esme looked around, shivering a little. It wasn't as cold in here as outside, but she couldn't stop the faint tremor down her spine. Dread perhaps. The sooner they spoke of this, the better.

Old furniture was stacked against the walls, a large Turkish rug covering the floor. Blade had little interest in fencing stolen goods but there were always people who needed coin desperately. He often traded coin or protection for the goods they offered. Charity here in the 'Chapel would have earned him naught more than a sneer.

Esme shivered. Her throat felt thick with unsaid words; *I didn't mean it, I was speaking of being your thrall, I should never have kissed you, friends…just friends*. All of it lies, but they were safe lies.

As she went to open her mouth, the thought spurred

something hot to life in her chest. She didn't want to be 'just friends' anymore, didn't want to take everything she'd said back. It was finally out in the air between them and though she was frightened of his lack of a response, a part of her wanted to confront him about it.

"You cold?" he asked quietly. His voice had always been deeper than most men; the kind of voice that sent shivers over her skin. He rarely ever raised it, but sometimes she wished she could sense what he was feeling in it. To yell or rage, just once.

But she knew why he didn't.

Esme nodded, her gaze settling on his throat and the corded muscle there as he swallowed. She wasn't quite brave enough to meet his eyes. "A little," she whispered.

Where was her courage now? Her defiant glee that the words were said? Rip took a step toward her, shrugging out of his leather coat and Esme couldn't stop herself from taking a step back. His shirt strained over the enormous slabs of muscle that decorated his chest, heavy braces indenting his shoulders. A workman's shirt; rough, coarse… But she knew the feel of it, the way it would abrade her skin.

As if she'd struck him, he froze.

And Esme realized that he thought she was frightened of him.

Stepping forward, she reached for his coat, twirling into it like a dancer. Rip's hands settled on her shoulders lightly as he helped her settle it in place, then lingered. With her back to him, Esme's heart suddenly raced. Slowly he gathered up her hair, hands so gentle she almost ached, and dragged it free of the collar. The ribbon she'd used to tie it back had loosened and Rip tugged it out, fingertips sliding through the silk of her hair.

"John?" she whispered.

"I like that," he murmured. "I 'ate it when you call me 'Rip'.

You're the only one who doesn't. The only one who sees me as John." A tentative finger wrapped around one of her black curls, gave a little tug. "You want to punish me? Aye, well you knew 'ow to do it."

Esme's fingers curled in the collar of the coat, holding it in place as she flinched. Suddenly her need to hurt him as he'd hurt her seemed nothing more than cruel. "I'm sorry."

A rough sigh. "So am I." Then the sensation of his body shifted behind her, leaving Esme feeling nothing but cold.

Rip stepped past, toward the lantern. Sinking down onto the dusty red rug, he tipped his chin at her. "Come. Sit by the light. Talk with me."

Her feet didn't want to move. Somehow she forced herself to cross the tense space, manoeuvring between dusty chairs and lamps. *Courage, Esme.* This wasn't the first battle she'd ever fought and it wouldn't be the last. But she felt almost sick to the stomach as she stiffly sank to her knees beside him. Clutching at his coat to hold it in place, her gaze dropped.

Rip shifted, drawing his hand back from his knee into the shadows of his body and she realized it was his mech hand. She'd been staring through it.

Reaching out, Esme caught it, feeling the cold of the metal beneath her palm. "Don't. You shouldn't hide it." The fingers flexed and hers slid between them, feeling the smooth ball-and-socket joins of each knuckle. It was rough work; the hydraulics in his forearm gleamed in the warm candlelight as he shifted, a piston hissing cool air against her skin. He'd never let her touch it before.

"Perhaps we should talk to Blade," she found herself saying, as though the weight of the silence would bury her. "Surely he can pay for a replacement. I've seen some of those new mech enhancements on the men fresh out of the Enclaves." Men who'd had to pay for their enhancements with years of service in the harsh steam-driven factories that weren't quite a prison. "They even have synthetic skin these days, though it never looks quite real enough–"

"Esme," he rumbled gruffly.

He wasn't here to talk about the hand.

Esme fell silent.

"Why didn't you tell me?"

She couldn't stop herself from looking up then, meeting his gaze helplessly. Every hopeless look over the years, every time she sought him out to sit with him, the teasing arguments in the kitchen as he taunted her and stole her ingredients... She'd turn around and her carrots would be missing, Rip protesting his innocence so skilfully that she couldn't help but laugh as she tried to find out where he'd hidden them. Pressing against him, her clever hands darting beneath his coat–though not entirely in search of whatever he'd stolen–until his cheeks would color and he'd present them with a flourish.

Baking his favourite lemon tart, just for him. Kissing his cheek when he brought her a new ribbon and wishing she had the courage to turn her lips to his. "I thought I did," she whispered.

Their fingers still interlinked. Rip gave a soft, bemused laugh. "You never said it. Never. I'd 'ave remembered."

"I thought I showed you—In everything that I did, in everything I said." Her cheeks heated. "I practically threw myself at you in the street the other day! And you pushed me away!"

His metal thumb stroked hers. Rip thought about her words for a moment, frowning slightly, the way he always did when he wanted to get his own words right. A man of caution. "Six months ago I wouldn't a pushed you away."

She watched his hand stroking hers. "What changed? What–"

And then she knew.

Esme's breath caught as their eyes met.

"I know I said I were right as a trivet." Pulling away, Rip scraped his metal hand over the back of his thickly muscled neck. "I told Blade I 'ad it under control. I just... I couldn't stand bein' trapped in the Warren anymore. I needed to get out. Start workin' again. I 'ate bein' useless." Those green eyes danced to hers and she saw the flare of hunger in them, his pupils dilating. A look just for her, that told her everything she ought to have known. A look that stripped her bare of the heavy velvet dress and left her feeling naked. "It ain't so bad, with other women. Just you. You throw me off the edge, Esme. I want you so much it 'urts. And then I can feel the 'unger creepin' up, threatenin' to take over. I don't want to 'urt you." He shook his head emphatically. "Never."

All this time she'd thought that he didn't want her. And he'd been afraid to lose control, to take her blood–or her body–for fear of hurting her. "Oh, John," she whispered. "I could have helped you. I've been a thrall for years. I know what to do. Sometimes Blade would–"

The vicious look he shot her stopped her in her tracks. The look of a man who wanted to hurt something–preferably his enemy. Esme slid closer, sliding her hand over his knee. "You have nothing to be jealous of," she reminded him. "It was only blood between me and Blade." Growing bold, she squeezed the hard muscle in his thigh as she knelt closer, digging her thumb in as she stroked the soft leather of his pants. Rip sucked in a sharp breath, his eyes glittering.

"So you do want me?" she asked, her whisper full of all manner of sin. "Just to clear up any misunderstandings?"

"Aye." Voice rough, his eyes dropping to her bodice. Rip let out a harsh breath. "Christ, I'm only a man."

Her hand slid lower, stroking the smooth leather over his thigh.

"Esme." A warning.

One she took no heed of. She felt light as a bird, a smile crossing her lips as she crept closer, pushing between his knees. *He wanted her.* The way a man wants a woman. The way a blue blood wanted his thrall. She was so happy she felt almost giddy.

"And when you spoke of me marrying tonight… were you speaking of someone else?"

Those green eyes glinted. "You'd be best off–"

"No." She put her finger to his lips. "I've had my share of misunderstandings. I won't suffer it anymore. Do you *want* me to marry another man?"

She read the answer on his face. Fierce, almost violent. Possessive. Esme shivered, her finger lightening against his lips. She let her hands drop to the buttons at her throat.

Esme slipped one of the buttons free. The red velvet frock-coat buttoned to her throat, but it fit her like a glove. And he noticed. She saw it on his face as he watched her undo several buttons, harsh hunger lighting his eyes with demonic need. Her nipples tightened, a fierce heat igniting deep in her belly. Her own hunger. Her own need. It had been years since she'd lain with her husband, and she wanted this man so much it hurt.

Every muscle in his body tensed, the leather creaking softly over his thighs. Still, he didn't reach for her, just looked up at her with that tight expression.

"Do you want to touch me?" Esme whispered, her knuckles brushing the smooth curve of her breasts as she worked the buttons lower. "Or perhaps… to taste me?"

That drew another heated glance that lit her on fire. She couldn't stop herself from reaching out, sliding her hands over the heavily muscled expanse of his shoulders. A groan wet her lips. "I want to touch *you*," she whispered, leaning closer. A light kiss against his throat. "I want to taste you–"

Her tongue darted out and licked the distended vein in his throat. His pulse kicked against her lips, racing hard. His body might be as still as a statue but he felt this. Tension practically vibrated in him.

"Esme, stop," he groaned. His hand clenched in her skirts as he hissed out a sharp breath, palm flattening over her bottom as he urged her against him.

She nipped his throat, drinking in the masculine scent she knew so well, the stubble of his jaw rasping against her cheek and lips. Hands darting, stroking, digging into the hard muscle as she pressed against him. This time she felt no sense of rejection at his words. She knew exactly what lay behind them.

Darting a glance at his eyes—they weren't black yet—she captured his face in her hands and slid into his lap. Her skirts rode up her thighs, bunching between her and his hips. Still, there wasn't enough fabric for her not to feel him.

"Oh." Esme's smile widened as she shifted against him, stockinged knees driving into the rug beneath them. This time there was no stopping her. She slid her hands over the roughened black stubble of his scalp and kissed him hard.

No hesitation. Not this time. Rip grabbed her, hauling her against his chest, his hips driving up into hers. Somewhere in the distance, rain began to patter on the roof.

"Want you," he growled. "Want you so damned much."

She tore her lips from his just long enough to gasp. "I want you too. I feel like I've wanted you forever."

Rip squeezed her against him fiercely, as if he couldn't quite reply. Then her hands were digging at his shirt, tugging it free of his pants. Fighting with his braces as she shoved them off his shoulders, her mouth greedy on his, tongue darting against his own. Finally she had the shirt free of his pants. Her palms flat against his rippled abdomen, she pushed him flat on his back and sucked in a ragged breath.

Rip fell back onto the rug on his elbows, not so much a sign of submission, but an acceptance... for now. The look in his eyes promised that she wouldn't have this chance again.

Esme didn't care. Her blood fired as she tore his shirt open, baring the heavy slab of his chest to her gaze. Smooth hairless skin met her gaze, the colour of honey. She'd always thought the warmth of his skin owed its colour to the sun, but though his hands and face were darker, his body was golden in the lamplight. One day he'd lose that, as the craving virus colonised and faded the colour from his skin. Or perhaps not. Ever since Honoria had discovered that her vaccinated blood lowered Blade's virus count, Esme had been thinking about asking for the vaccination herself. To keep her man as human as he could possibly be, with the virus raging in him.

Thick muscle, his abdomen chiselled as it narrowed down to his hips. She couldn't stop looking. She didn't think she'd ever want to stop touching him.

"Esme." He drew the folds of his shirt together, as if unnerved by her stare.

Esme caught his hands. "Don't," she said. "I want to look at you. I love your body." Her fingernails dug into his abdomen. "All of you. All mine." Leaning down she kissed him again, lips tracing his own. He would never be hand-some in the way society dictated, but she loved the way he looked. Hard, powerful, full of a dangerous, feral grace. A man. Not like those dandies of the Echelon, who padded their coats or wore girdles. Rip was solid muscle.

Slowly she kissed his cheek, tongue tracing the heavy scar through his eyebrow. Rip's breath came hard, his hips flexing beneath her.

"You don't know what you do to me," he whispered.

Sliding a hand between them, she cupped it around the heavy length of his erection. "I've some idea."

"If you don't stop that, I'm gonna 'ave you on your back," Rip breathed.

Tempting. She looked up and he saw it in her eyes. His own narrowed, darkness leeching out from the pupils as if to swallow his irises. The hunger.

Catching her hips, he rolled them and Esme fell back with a breathless laugh. Pinning her wrists to the rug, he loomed over her, his hips resting between hers. Careless of the fall of her skirts, she locked her legs around his hips, her stockings gliding against the smooth leather of his trousers.

Black eyes met hers. The hunger in all its ascendancy. Esme lay still, surrendering to him completely. Knowing how to control the fierce fury within him.

For long seconds, he breathed in harshly, clenching his eyes shut as if to fight it. Esme simply relaxed, letting him control her. The desire for sex and blood warred within him. She just had to give it a little push in the right direction.

"Touch me," she whispered, arching her back just enough to press her hips against his. The friction made her breath catch. "I want your hands on me."

His eyes met hers; demon-black. "Where?"

"Undo my buttons."

The complexity of the task made him focus. Esme slid her hands over his neck, luxuriating in the feel of his knuckles against her skin as he slipped each button free. The frock-coat tugged open, her shirt-waist pressed tight against her skin.

Rip leaned down and brushed his mouth against hers. She could feel the tremors in his body, the rigid steel of his arms as he held himself immobile. Slowly he divested her of the shirt, leaving only a corset and shift. The scent of her violet water grew stronger as he undid the busk that ran down the front of her corset and Esme gasped against his lips as his hand curved over her breast.

"Yes," she whispered, her hips flexing against his.

Slow. Gentle. Torturous. Rip lowered his mouth to her throat, but only briefly. With a sharp exhale he swiftly moved lower, his lips trailing over the curve of each plump breast, lips dragging her shift lower. Tugging it down, his tongue darted over her nipple as he slowly suckled it into his mouth.

Esme groaned. It had been so long since she'd been touched that she couldn't remember if it had ever felt as good as this. Teeth rasped over her nipple and she couldn't hold still any more.

"John," she whispered. "Oh, God, John. I want you. Now." Darting a hand between them she reached for the buttons on his trousers.

Rip shook her away. "No," he rasped. "Need to be in control. Just lemme–" He took her mouth again, breathing hard against her lips. "Lemme go slow."

The rain rattled on the tin roof. She should have been cold but Esme barely noticed the chill against her naked skin. All she could see was Rip, his shoulders blotting out the entire world. All she could feel were his fingers, sliding down her skirts and dragging them up. Fist bunching in the velvet.

The chill bit at her legs, but she moaned into his mouth, cupping his cheeks and kissing him breathlessly. His hands slid over her stockings and Esme spread her thighs. "*Yes.*" A gasp.

Fingers trembled on her garter, then the smooth skin of her inner thigh. When he found the damp cotton of her draws he let out another rough exhale. Tugging them open, finding her, wet and ready and arching beneath him...

It was bliss. Esme moaned, turning her head and sinking her teeth into the flesh of his shoulder as his fingertips darted over her heated flesh. White light exploded behind her eyes, the world disappearing until all that remained was

Rip and the dull roar of the rain on the roof. Her body trembling, trembling... On the precipice.

Then his hand was gone. Esme blinked. *No.*

"Get this off." He paused and tugged at her drawers. Fighting them free. She caught one last glimpse of the black of his eyes, then he shoved both hands under her bottom and slid lower.

The wet heat of his mouth almost made her scream. Esme jerked, her fingers sinking into the hard muscle of his shoulders. Tracing the steel of his mech limb. She bit her lip as he tongued her, hard and deep, suckling on her clitoris and bringing her to the edge again with ruthless determination.

Esme shattered. It took her hard, leaving her panting and breathless, Rip pulling back to drag in his own shuddering breath. She flinched as his fingertips trailed down her thigh, so sensitive and wrung out that she could scarcely bear it. "Oh God, oh God," she whispered, again and again.

Rip slid up her body, dragging her into his arms. She felt like crying again, as if he'd utterly destroyed her. And then she was and he tugged her tighter, locking her face against his chest as if he could hide her from the world. "Easy luv," he whispered, pressing a kiss to her hair. He breathed out a rough laugh. "Makin' a man think he's done ought wrong."

"No." She curled her fingers in his shirt and glanced up, tears spiking her lashes together. "That was amazing. I just... I just..."

A slow smile curled over his lips. "Aye. Overwhelmed are you?"

Esme nodded, pressing her lips to his throat. She could feel the hardness of his erection between them. This wasn't finished yet. Sliding her hand between them she cupped him through his pants.

Rip sucked in a sharp breath and rolled her onto her back, coming over her. Resting on his elbows, he toyed with her hair, staring down at her with a look of sharp longing on his face. "I want to," he admitted hoarsely. "Want you so much."

"But?" she whispered, hearing the unspoken word.

Rip shut his black eyes with a shudder. "I could barely control meself through that," he admitted. "I can't risk it, Esme. Not yet."

"I trust you," she said, stroking his face.

He shuddered. "I can't, Esme. *I can't.*"

The ache of need was almost unbearable. Frustration snaked through her. But she could feel the tense line in his shoulders as she stroked her hands up over his shirt-covered back, soothing and whispering under her breath.

"I'll wait," she whispered. "I'll wait for you, John. Always."

I'LL WAIT FOR YOU.

Something twisted tight in Rip's chest, like a man's hand closing over his heart. Hope? An incredulous disbelief? *A cur like you couldn't be that lucky.* But that was his mother's pimp's voice he heard. He had to believe he deserved this, that Esme could truly be his. Otherwise he'd have ended up staring at the world through a bottle years ago, with Whitey's voice echoing in his ears.

Rip curled against her, tucking her bodice up and making sure she was warm. She was so small against him, her breathing settling as she fell asleep. Rip listened to the rain softening on the roof. He felt like the luckiest man alive.

There was only one thing that marred his happiness.

If he couldn't learn to control himself, then he might never be able to give Esme what she wanted most. She'd said she would wait, but how long? He hadn't lied when he'd claimed that she'd be happiest as someone's wife, someone's mother.

She was almost five-and-thirty. Long past her best child-bearing days. What if he couldn't give her children before it was too late? What if it took him years to control himself enough? Blade had admitted that it had been years before he himself could feed directly from the vein without taking too much, though he'd had no one to teach him how to control the craving.

Rip hugged her tighter, pressing a kiss to her hair. He'd speak to her about it. But not now. Christmas was only a few days away and he knew how much she'd been looking forward to it. Once it was over, he would sit her down and offer her the chance to stop this before it was too late for both of them.

Even if it would kill a part of him inside.

CHAPTER 9

*T*here were three days until Christmas. Then two. And then one.

The men spent most of their time hunting through Undertown and keeping guard on the rookery whilst Annie recovered. Esme busied herself with the other women and the children, preparing the Warren for its first Christmas.

There were no signs of it in the heart of the city where the Echelon ruled, but traces of jollity sprouted everywhere in the East End.

Mistletoe seemed to dangle from every rafter in the Warren; Esme quite suspected whose hand had done that when she saw Blade laughingly snatch another kiss from Honoria. Indeed, he'd managed to lure both her and Rip beneath it once or twice. Neither of them had mentioned what had happened that night and it irritated Blade to no end.

"I only want what's best for you, Es," he'd lecture her.

"I know what's best for me," she would reply with a straight face as she bustled about her work. Only when she turned away would she give herself the opportunity to smile as

Blade sighed in exasperation behind her. There was no surer way to get at him than to keep something from him.

Every night she would sneak into Rip's room in her nightgown and fall asleep in his arms. Of the other, though he gave her as much pleasure as he could, he would never let her touch him.

Her smile faded slightly as she stuffed the goose, ready for the morning. It would happen. When Rip was no longer afraid he'd hurt her. Still, she couldn't shake the feeling that he wasn't quite telling her something.

CHRISTMAS CAME in a blaze of white. It had snowed again during the night and Esme woke in Rip's arms, watching the drift of it through his glass window.

"'Ave to get a bigger bed," he murmured, snuggling his face against her hair.

"I don't know," she replied, burying herself in his arms. "I quite like this one." Lifting her head, she pressed a kiss to his lips. His eyelashes fluttered open. "Merry Christmas."

A slow smile spread over his mouth making Esme's heart flutter. "Why so it is," he drawled. "Do you want your present?"

"It depends on what it is," she replied with a naughty little smile.

Rip's eyes darkened. "Wench." Spilling her onto her stomach with a laugh, he reached over her and dragged something out from underneath the bed. The press of his body drove her into the mattress and Esme almost moaned.

"'Ere," he said, handing a small, brightly wrapped box to her. "Your other present's downstairs, under the tree, but I wanted to give you this before…"

Before anyone else could see.

Esme sat up, the blankets pooling in her lap. Her heart stammered as she reached for the small box. It was jewellery. It had to be. And though she told herself not to expect anything, she couldn't help remembering the way he'd spoken of marriage.

"What is it?" she whispered.

"Open it." His smile was almost gleeful and she realised he'd probably never done anything like this before.

Tugging off the bright paper, she opened the velvet box. Then gasped. A small silver 'E' winked in the light with a strip of black velvet to tie around the throat.

"D'you like it?"

"Oh, John," she whispered. "It's perfect." Her trembling fingertips stroked the letter. She'd never been given anything of the like.

Reaching up, she kissed him on the lips, feeling the chafe of his stubble against her cheeks. Rip smiled in a lazy manner, then captured her face in both hands, the cool steel of his mech limb a startling sensation. He kissed her deeply, turning it hot and hard, his tongue caressing hers. Esme melted against him with a soft moan.

It was over before it began. Rip drew back, his forehead resting against hers as he fought to capture his breath. Esme stroked his chest. "Let me please you," she whispered. "I could–"

"No." He pulled away, his face expressionless. Blackness gleamed in his eyes; the hunger.

A sharp ache filled Esme's chest. The fierce need shouldn't have roused so quickly. Rip had better control than this. Unless it was true... unless she was his Achilles heel. And always would be.

"I'll wait," she whispered, sinking onto her knees. She pasted a small smile on her lips as she squeezed his hand. "Thank you for my present."

Rip looked away. Shuttered. She almost felt like reaching out, to ask if that was the only thing bothering him. "Aye," he said. "Weren't much. But you ought to 'ave pretty things o' your own. Come. I can 'ear people stirrin'."

———

THE MOMENT ESME tried to put her apron on, Rip tugged it off. Balling it in his fist he threw it at Will's chest. "Apron's yours, lass," he called.

A slow smile curled over Will's mouth. "But pink suits your colourin' so much better," he shot back, then tossed it at Rip's face.

Blade snatched it out of the air midway and slung it around his hips. "Don't want to get me waistcoat mucky," he said, flicking imaginary lint off the red velvet waistcoat. With a devilish wink, he dragged the pan with the goose off the bench and headed for the oven.

"What's going on?" Esme laughed breathlessly.

A second later she squealed as Rip slung her up over his shoulder, one hand planted firmly on her backside. "Thought you ought to 'ave the day off," he said, the rumble of his baritone shivering beneath her hips. "We'll prepare lunch."

"But you don't know what you're doing!"

Rip swung her through the door into the sitting room with Honoria and Lena looking up in surprise at their appearance. Esme's cheeks burned.

"'elped you enough times. I swear I won't burn the duck."

"It's a goose!" Esme slid down his body as he dangled her over a stuffed armchair. Arms sliding around his neck, she stared into his eyes as her toes found the edge of the armchair. The press of his body did wicked things to her breath. Hard against her softness.

He felt it too, green embers of heat flickering to life in his eyes. A slow, devastating smile curled over his mouth. "Why look at that," he murmured, his gaze lifting. "Mistletoe."

Esme glanced up. "How convenient," she whispered.

When she looked back down their eyes met. Slowly he reached forward and pressed a chaste kiss to her lips, his cool breath teasing her. The brief dart of his tongue wet her lips and Esme softened, sinking against him. She wanted him so much, though she couldn't forget the other people in the room.

Rip drew back, a look of knowing smouldering in his half-closed eyes. "*Later,*" he mouthed.

Esme let her arms drop and found her balance on the armchair. "Don't you burn my goose," she said, trying to recover her breath. "Or the beef haunch." Her face blanched. "You'll need to get that in the oven first. Tell Blade to take–"

Rip backed away. "Sit," he admonished. "Drink some mulled wine and relax." There was a challenge in his eyes. "That's an order."

Esme gave in. As Rip left the room, she exchanged a helpless look with Honoria.

Honoria held up her hands. "I've been banished too." A wicked look filled her eyes. "Though I find myself quite pleased about the circumstances now. *What* a curious development."

She wasn't speaking of the goose.

"Lena," Honoria barely turned her head. "Why don't you go and drag Charlie and Lark out of bed. It's past time for them to be up."

With a sigh Lena climbed to her feet. "I'm not a child, you know. Why can't I stay to help interrogate Esme? I daresay I'll do a better job of it than you. After all..." She flashed Esme a saucy smile. "I've been aware of it for weeks."

Honoria arched a brow and Lena held her hands up in defeat. "Fine."

"Now," Honoria said, getting up and filling a glass with mulled wine as Lena thundered up the stairs. She handed it to Esme. "What haven't you been telling Blade? He's desperate to know what's going on."

Esme accepted the glass with a sigh of resignation. "Promise you won't tell him?"

Honoria's smile widened. "Only if you tell me everything."

So Esme did.

The morning passed in a fury of giggles and whispering, with Lena, Tin Man and the children venturing forth to feel the shape of the wrapped boxes under the tree. Meggie had decided to stay with her mother in the bedroom, as Annie was still too stricken to leave her bed.

Esme curled back into the armchair, the mulled wine easing her senses until she barely gave her kitchen a thought.

Dinner was served with a flourish, Blade bowing at the head of the table as he removed her pink apron and tossed it aside with gusto. Carving the goose and the beef–both nicely browned but not overcooked–turned into a theatre act until Honoria laughingly took the knife off Blade and handed it to Rip. Rip finished the carving with swift economy.

"Here," Blade called, lifting his glass of blood and mimicking the precise tones of the Echelon, "is to our very first Christmas."

Everybody raised their glasses.

"An entirely heathen practice," Blade continued, in mockingly perfect English, "but one I could quite continue." He glanced down with a warm smile as he lost the accent. "You'll 'ave to thank 'onoria, for 'twas 'er father's practice to celebrate with their family. And I thought, considerin' our family's recently grown larger, that we ought to start our own traditions. So without further ado–"

"Of course there'll be further ado," Honoria interrupted, "for we know you too well."

Blade grinned at her. "'ere's to the family."

"Hear, hear," the group around the table echoed.

Glasses clinked, plates were handed around and everyone set to eating.

"'ow is it?" Rip asked, easing one arm along the back of Esme's chair.

"Delicious," she replied with a sidelong glance as she tasted the goose. "Almost... succulent."

His gaze heated as he nursed his wine glass in his hand, blood staining the clear glass. "That's because I made sure you got the breast."

"That used to be your favourite part," she replied innocently, taking another bite of the goose. "A shame you no longer partake."

"It still is me favourite part," he murmured, his fingers stretching out and brushing the back of her neck. "And I *do* intend to partake. Most thoroughly."

Leaning forward, he brought her fork to his lips and bit into a steaming piece of meat. "You're right. It's delicious."

Esme pushed him away with a laugh, noting the sharp glance Blade threw her, his curiosity rampant. Honoria smuggled a smile at his side.

The afternoon passed by in a happy blur. The children cleared the plates and Rip made sure her glass was always full. Too full sometimes. She couldn't stop smiling, especially as the presents were handed round. Rip's gift proved to be a perfectly innocent copy of Vanity Fair, and he smiled as he handed it to her, no doubt thinking of the necklace he'd given her.

Blade's gifts were extravagant and drew gasps, though Lena's gifts drew the most attention. She'd once apprenticed with a clockmaker and her skill with cogs and gears had created amazing clockwork toys for the children. Even Meggie came down to play with them, summoning the occasional smile as a little metal mouse dashed around the floor in circles. Esme drew the little girl into her lap and rested her chin against her hair, breathing in the sweet little-girl smell.

Blade eased next to her on the sofa, stretching out to tug at Meggie's curls. The little girl clapped a hand to her head and looked up.

"Look what I found in your 'air," he said, holding out a paper-wrapped chocolate with feigned innocence.

Meggie took it with a smile and Blade directed her to a bowl of sweets on the table.

The second interrogation had arrived.

Esme lounged back on the sofa, watching him languidly.

"You look... 'appy."

"I am," she replied. "This was a smashing idea, Blade."

"Aye." His gaze roved the room, watching everyone he ruled over with a certain proudness. "Thought we all deserved some cheer after the year we've 'ad." His gaze darkened. "Losin' O'Shea to the vampire and nearly Rip too... And 'onoria, losin' her father like that."

Esme followed his gaze to where his wife curled sleepily in a chair. "She looks content."

Blade smile softened—answer enough. Then he turned and cut her a direct glance. "Considerin' you ain't stripped skin off me 'ide for the other night, I take it the two o' you've reconciled?"

Her gaze lowered to her wineglass. "Perhaps I'm merely plotting my revenge."

"Do you remember," he asked lightly, "when you stole 'onor's diaries? I believe the term I used then was meddlin'."

"I would much prefer it if you didn't," she told him firmly.

Blade smiled, knowing he'd been forgiven. "Are you goin' to tell me what's goin' on?"

"Rip and I have reached a compromise," she replied, standing up. "And that is all I'm going to say."

"You're a devil, Esme."

She shot him a smile as she crossed the room.

Hours later, the children began to drift upstairs to bed.

"I'm goin' up too." Rip stretched nonchalantly, his eyes meeting hers for just a second before he glanced away. That second was enough to scorch all the way through her.

Esme looked down into her cup of tea as he stood. She could feel Blade's eyes on them both. She'd take her time in the kitchen, let Rip retire long before she snuck up the stairs herself. Putting aside her tea cup, she nodded to him. "Have a good night's sleep."

His eyes twinkled. "I will."

Sweeping into the kitchen, Esme listened to the sound of chatter behind her as she surveyed the mess. The tea had helped to clear her head, but she didn't quite feel up to cleaning up.

Who cared if Blade saw her? Time to relax, to go up to bed and perhaps see how far she could push her lover...

Still, old habits died hard and Esme took the pair of old milk bottles out to place by the arch in the brickwork that led out into the lane behind the Warren. They would be collected in the morning and the task wouldn't wait.

Bending down, she nestled the milk bottles in the old crate left there to be collected. Noise whispered in the slushy snow of the street and Esme jerked her head up, staring into the dark.

"Hello?" she called. "Is there anybody there?"

Only the gentle hush of drifting snowflakes answered her. Still, she couldn't quite escape the sensation that she wasn't alone.

Her heartbeat ratcheted up and Esme dragged her shawl

close around her shoulders. Taking one nervous step back, she kept looking around.

Movement shifted behind her, a hand clapping over her mouth and wrenching her head back. She was jerked hard against a man's lanky body, something sharp pressing into her throat and stilling the scream that boiled there.

Esme froze.

"That's right, dove," a man whispered in guttural cockney slang. He stank of rot, as if he'd crawled straight from the graveyard himself. Or perhaps he worked with some form of death? "Make a sound and I'll cut yer throat, you understan'?"

Esme nodded carefully. What could she do? As her eyes rolled, she caught a glimpse of the warm light glowing in the windows of her kitchen. So close to safety...

And yet so far...

Hot breath stirred over her ear and her attacker's hand relaxed, though didn't quite leave her lips. "Name's Bill 'iggins and I been meanin' to 'ave a little word with you." He laughed roughly. "Your menfolk think they're so smart, don't they? Aye, well they ought to watch their backs a little closer." A hand slid over her breasts, making her jerk. He laughed again, the sound like gravel. "And 'ere's me, stealin' their little ladybird right out from under their noses. Ain't so clever now, are they?"

Hot wet tears slid down her cheeks as he kissed her throat. The hook dug into the tender flesh there and something warm slid down into her collarbone. Higgins licked at it, suckling the skin tenderly and making her cringe. Under her skirts, she scraped a H into the snow, moving slowly and carefully. Then the E and the L.

"Now, you come wit' me and keep quiet," he whispered. "Let's get a little better acquainted, shall we?"

She never got the chance to trace the letter P.

CHAPTER 10

*R*ip relaxed back in bed, cupping his head in his hand. His mech arm lay cold and motionless on the bed beside him. Staring at the ceiling, he listened to each creak as people sought their beds, his breath catching at each sound then releasing when he realised it wasn't Esme.

The house fell still.

Nothing but silence, his ears almost ringing as he tried to listen to her. His rooms were directly above the kitchen, and though he could usually hear her moving about down there – indeed, he'd spent many a night listening to her – there was no sound now.

She wouldn't have gone to her own bed, would she?

Rip frowned. That look he'd given her had spoken volumes and the little smile she'd tried to hide was as much a reply as anything she could have uttered.

He swung his legs out of bed and reached for his shirt. Dressing swiftly, he eased open the door to his room and went searching for her.

Not in her room. Nor the lower section of the house. The kitchen hearth glowed in the shadows, Esme's apron lying forlornly on the bench. Rip picked it up, but the material was cold. An uneasy prickling ran over the back of his neck.

The back door rattled under his touch. Locked. She couldn't be out there. Turning, he raked his gaze over the kitchen as if it would tell him where she was.

What did she do usually? Her pans were all put away, some still resting in the sink for tomorrow. Yanking open the door that led to the basement and the ice-room where Blade kept their blood chilled, he tried to scent her. Nothing.

Perhaps she'd fallen? He hurried down the stairs but there was no sign of her. The drumbeat of his heart started to kick a little harder.

"Esme?" he whispered, but nobody answered him.

Raking a hand over the stubble on his scalp he climbed back up to the kitchen. Footsteps creaked on the main stairs that led upwards and he let out a relieved breath. Finally.

Shoving through into the living room, he stopped in his tracks as Blade slowed, eyeing him curiously from the stairs.

"What are you doin' up?" Blade asked.

"You ain't seen Esme?" he asked, his chest tightening. "She ain't been with you?" It wasn't expected now that Blade took his blood from Honoria, but it was worth the question.

Blade shook his head. "No. Ain't seen 'er." His voice hardened. "Why?"

"She were s'posed to stay with me tonight," Rip blurted. "I can't find 'er."

Blade's knuckles tightened on the stair rails as they stared at each other. "She were in the kitchen," he said finally. "Puttin' stuff away last I saw 'er. You keep searchin'. I'll rouse the lads, see if anyone saw 'er."

His tone remained even but Rip saw the look in his master's eyes and it chilled him to the core.

Blade thundered up the stairs and Rip turned back to the kitchen. Maybe she'd been locked out? Blade or one of the lads often performed a last check on all the doors before they went to bed. He yanked it open and stared out into the yard.

Snow gleamed in the moonlight, soft flakes drifting down. Enough for him to see the faint swishing trail of someone's skirts.

Rip strode outside, his nerves itching along his skin. From the faintness of the impression, she'd been outside long enough for the snow to begin filling it.

The milk bottles were all stacked neatly in their crate. He knelt down in the shadow of the arch, fingertips pressing into a strange line. Almost… a letter. Thank God Esme had taught him to read somewhat. He traced the H with a frown. H. E. And something else that had been almost obliterated by her skirts. I? L?

H. E. L…

His blood ran cold. *Help.* With a surge of his thighs he straightened and stepped out into the back lane. There was no one in sight, but the trail of her skirts dragged toward the street. Rip took three steps before he smelt it.

Blood.

A little droplet of blood in the snow.

"Blade!" He was running before he knew it, his lungs seizing in his chest. *No, no, no.* This was his worst nightmare. He knew immediately what had happened and how. Higgins. This was just what the vindictive prick would do now that Rip and Blade had killed several of his men.

The thought made him feel sick. Not Esme. Anyone but Esme. Why the hell hadn't she screamed? The only reason she wouldn't have, would be if she couldn't.

Panting, he staggered into the street. Wheel ruts and foot-steps turned the snow into slush, Esme's trail vanishing in with the echo of a thousand others. Rip spun on his heel, though he knew what he'd find. He'd been in bed for almost half an hour. More than enough time to vanish with her if someone knew how.

Fuck. He scraped his hands over his head. Not a soul lingered in the streets and the curtains were closed on most of the windows. He'd waste his time – and breath – in questioning people. Whitechapel was the sort of place where nobody ever saw anything.

"Rip?" Blade slowed down at the end of the lane, Will hard on his heels. "You seen 'er?"

He shook his head, his throat so thick he could barely talk. Heat wet his eyes. *"No."* The word came out hoarse and barely audible. He tried again. "It's that Slasher. I know it. I saw some blood on the snow back there--" He lost the ability to speak again, his throat closing over completely.

"Aye," Blade murmured, clapping a hand on his shoulder. "Well, 'e's made 'is mistake this time." Eyes glittering, he surveyed the street. "We'll get 'er back, Rip. I swear. And then I'll skin 'im alive for this."

AN HOUR LATER, they met again at the junction of Petticoat Lane. Rip was drenched in the icy chill water of the sewers, shaking so hard he could barely stand. The rage in him was growing, the hunger creeping over him like the threatening weight of an avalanche. The only thing holding it at bay was the thought that if he lost control, he'd never find her. He needed to be rational for this.

"No sign?" Blade asked.

"Chemical," he managed to choke out, his throat and nose burning from the smell of it. He felt like he'd never get the scent out of his nose. Something he'd smelt before, only he couldn't quite place it now... "One o' those chemical bombs they been usin'."

Will knelt in the snow, his amber eyes gleaming in the moonlight. As close to the edge as Rip in his own way. "Found nothin'," he growled in frustration, his own eyes red-rimmed. "Every tunnel stinks o' chemical. Can't smell a bleedin' thing now."

"'E planned this," Blade muttered, staring down the street. "Knew what our strengths are. 'Ow we work. *Fuck.*"

"What you want us to do?" Will asked. "Rouse the streets? See if anything saw something?"

"That'll take 'ours," Rip snapped. And Esme didn't have that long.

How long had it take Higgins to get her back to his hidden lair? How long to strap her to his table, to insert the needles in her veins that would slowly steal her life away? How long until she was nothing more than a dry husk of the woman she'd once been?

Rip spun and kicked at a pile of boxes against the corner, sending scraps and rubbish flying. The streets became black and white; the colour of a graveyard.

Someone caught his mech wrist and he spun, prepared to lash out. Will caught his fist before it could land, yanking his arm up behind him and Rip glared into the face of his master.

"She needs you," Blade said, letting his mech hand go. "Rein yourself in. *Now.*"

Rip shut his eyes and sucked in a sharp breath. *Wanted to kill. Wanted to tear something apart, anything to stop this helpless, goddamned terror.* His shoulders slumped as the anger and fury washed out of him. Blade was right. He was no help to Esme in this condition.

Blinking, the colour of the world snapping back in on him again, he turned to glare up into Will's burning gaze. "I'm fine."

Will let him go and stepped back out of reach. "Someone's

got to know where Higgin's hides. If he's a slasher, he'll be sellin' the blood down at them drainin' factories. Someone there buys it on the sly; they'll know how to contact him."

"Go," Blade snapped. "And be quick about it. I'll 'unt down below again, see if I can make out any scent trail. Maybe that chemical's wearin' off." He nodded at Rip. "You joinin' me?"

Chemical.

Rip stared at him. "Where's he getting' the chemical from?" He took a step back, his mind suddenly reeling. *Getting hard to find bodies, Rip.* The sudden memory of Dr. Creavey's examination room sprang to mind. And the breath-stealing scent of whatever he'd used to preserve those specimens in all of the jars.

The woman on the examination table, her wrists slit and her body eerily pale. Like she'd been drained of life. Rip swore under his breath. Under his nose all along and he'd not realised until now.

What better way to hide the drained bodies than to give them to someone who'd make sure they were never seen again? And would probably pay for them in the process.

"Got an idea," he snarled. "I'm goin' to visit an old friend."

Blade nodded. "Move quick and watch your back. I'll be in Undertown."

"Aye." They all nodded at each other.

"You see somethin' and you whistle," Blade said, referring to the whistle's that would pierce through each of their hearing from miles away. Nothing human would hear them, but the sound would set dogs barking and went through Rip like an ice-pick to the brain.

"If you find nothin', then we'll meet back 'ere in an 'our," Rip said, praying under his breath that he wouldn't see them again until Esme was found.

Rip stepped back and placed a solid kick to the middle of the door. The wood splintered with a satisfying bang and he shoved his way through. "Creavey?" he bellowed. "You in 'ere?"

A light flickered to life as someone hurriedly lit a lantern. Rip's predator gaze focused on it with deathly intensity. He was moving before he thought, shoving through the door into Creavey's personal chambers.

Photographs littered the walls. Grainy pictures of bodies on examination tables and the jars in Creavey's lab. Rip looked away in disgust and found his prey cowering by a stuffed armchair in his stained nightgown. The lantern burned on a small table, next to a book on dissection and a pot of tea.

"Christ," Creavey snapped. "You scared me half to death, Rip. What are you doing here at this hour?"

Rip strode forward and grabbed the doctor by the throat. He slammed him up against the wall, photos fluttering like dying moths to the floor as he snarled.

"Where you been gettin' your bodies from?" he snapped. "You been givin' someone vials o' that formalde'yde?"

The colour drained out of Creavey's face. "Don't know what you're… talking about…" he choked out.

Rip leaned forward, his mech fingers closing tighter as Creavey made a strangled sound. "Gettin' 'ard to find bodies," he snapped. "That's what you said and I saw that girl what I thought done 'erself in. Drained o' blood. You still got 'er? I'd be curious to know if there's any needle marks in her elbows, or more slashes across her throat and thighs. That's ow they do it." He slammed Creavey back against the wall. "That's what the Slashers do when they tie someone down."

Suddenly he pictured Esme lying there on Creavey's examination table, her body pale and faint bloody marks across her wrist. *No. He wouldn't be too late. He wouldn't.* The thought tore through him like a knife and as he blinked he realized Creavey was turning purple.

Rip let him go and stepped back as the man slumped to the floor, sucking in breath through his badly bruised throat. He knelt down, staring into the man's terrified eyes. "Now, I don't got a lot o' time. Nor patience." Blackness flickered behind his vision but he reined it in. *Later.* "You know Blade's 'ousekeeper?"

Creavey nodded sharply.

"The slashers got 'er," Rip said in a quiet, deadly-soft voice. "And I want 'er back. A man by the name o' Higgins 'iggins. You 'eard o' 'im? You know where 'e dwells?"

The stink of urine flooded through the room. "Can't," Creavey gasped. "Said he'd kill me if I said anything."

The blackness obliterated everything. The next thing Rip knew, Creavey was screaming as Rip shoved him down onto one of the frigid steel examination tables in the laboratory. Pinning him by the throat, he yanked a small rolling table closer, with its tray of evil-looking instruments.

"'e's got my woman," he heard himself say. "And you think 'e's the greater danger at the moment?" His hand closed over something sharp. He held it up. "'e might kill you. Some'd say that'd be a mercy to what I intend."

As Creavey screamed, Rip held the gadget up. A small, razor-sharp wheel of some description. He wound the crank attached to the shaft of it and the razor suddenly started spinning, light glinting off its edges.

"Now me," he whispered. "I don't plan on killin' you at all. Not at first."

Creavey's fingers wrapped around the cold steel of his mech hand. "I'll... tell..." Froth bubbled on his lips as his gaze locked on the gadget Rip held.

Rip stepped back.

The doctor scrambled off the table, into the corner of the

room where he cowered. "I couldn't get the bodies." He started crying. "Metaljackets started patrolling the cemeteries at nights. What was I to do?"

Rip stared at him. How any man could do such a vile thing was beyond him. He flung the circular saw aside. "So you started buyin' them from the cursed Slashers?" He kicked the rolling table aside and metal implements scattered everywhere. "Knowin' what they do to people?"

"It's easier to examine the tissues," Creavey whispered. "Without all the blood in the body."

A vein in Rip's temple throbbed. "Where is 'e?"

"I don't know," Creavey sobbed. "I don't. I swear I don't! I just deliver the formaldehyde to the back of an apothecary in Bethnal Green. They've got the bodies there, hidden in a shed out the back. I think... I think there's a tunnel down into Undertown in the shed."

Thoughts raced through his brain; a map of the streets thereabouts. "By apothecary, do you mean opium den?"

Creavey nodded.

Heavily defended by one of the gangs as run that part of town. Rip's fist clenched. "Don't you go leavin' the area," he snapped. "I still got words to 'ave with you."

Then he turned and left the doctor quivering behind him.

CHAPTER 11

"*N*o!" Esme kicked as the man shoved her back against the gurney. "No!"

She screamed as he wrenched her arm back and tightened a leather strap around it.

The room was dank and cold, hidden deep in Undertown. They'd passed dozens of Slashers on the way, splashing colourless liquid all through the tunnels from enormous glass jars. The stench of it took her breath and she knew what its purpose was.

No one would be able to track her by scent. Not Blade. Not Will. Not even Rip.

She'd picked at the cotton on her sleeves to try and leave threads behind, but the sewers were dark and the water washed away the cotton. As Higgins wrenched her through a tunnel, Esme had ripped the black satin from her throat and curled her hand around the small silver 'E' until she found a suitable spot. Then she'd deliberately tripped and dropped the necklace just before Higgins shoved her deep into the tunnel system that spawned his home.

"Stay still," Higgins snarled, waving the hook on his hand at her in warning.

Her fright of it had long since faded. If he managed to strap her down, he'd kill her anyway. She kicked out and Higgins staggered back into a tray of rusted implements. He looked up at her with a murderous gleam in her eye and Esme rolled, trying to yank at the strap on her left wrist.

The hook sank into the steel table an inch from her nose and Esme screamed and jerked back. Higgins loomed over her and grabbed her right wrist, strapping it down with brutal efficiency.

"I'd kill you for that," he said, then suddenly laughed. "But we're goin' to do that anyways. And I always says, waste not, want not."

Yanking at her skirts, he caught one of her ankles and stretched it out. Esme squirmed. The leather straps around her wrists had no give in them. Her heart thundered. *No. Please no… Not like this.*

Gutters ran along the edges of the table to a hole at the end where a tube siphoned whatever liquid splashed through into an enormous glass vial that stood in the corner, almost her height. The bottom of it was nestled into a gleaming copper machine.

Esme yanked again, her eyes streaming with tears. Rip. Where was Rip? She was so frightened she could hardly breathe, but she knew he'd come for her. As soon as he realised she was missing…

What if he'd fallen asleep? Or thought she wanted to sleep in her own bed? Esme yanked again and the buckle that she'd loosened on her left wrist slipped a fraction of an inch.

She stilled, watching as Higgins turned to the tray of implements. A little hunchback watched from the corner, eyes gleaming avidly at her. Esme didn't dare move. The ugly little creature hadn't spoken so far, but if it saw that the strap had loosened fractionally, it might raise the alarm.

There'd only be one chance at this.

Higgins picked up a glass hypodermic syringe with a long hollow needle. She'd seen the like before. Tom's mother had frequently injected herself with morphia or opium-tinctures to ease her gout.

The slashers had corrupted the syringe however, using it to draw blood instead of injecting. A rubber tube stretched from the end of it, toward the collecting device in the corner. "Modo, crank the filtration-device," Higgins commanded.

The hunchback darted for the machine and set his enormous hands on the crank. He started turning it, his face straining with the effort. It sped up and then the boiler-pack sputtered. Higgins flicked open an air vent and the boiler coughed to life as oxygen hit the small coal-fire inside. The whole thing vibrated as the hunchback stopped turning the crank.

The noise was horrendous. Esme tried to slide her wrist out of the leather loop as the pair of them watched the device, but it caught on the fleshy part of her hand. Not quite loose enough.

Come on. She yanked again, getting nowhere. No matter where she looked her gaze kept lingering on the tray with its vicious array of implements; the syringes hooked to the filtration device, sharp razors for slashing at the veins and an enormous cleaver. She knew what that was for. Getting rid of any bodies the slashers didn't want to draw unwelcome attention back to them.

"Nearly ready," Higgins muttered, raking his hook over the gleaming glass canister with a steely shriek. He glanced at her. "A pity we're in such an 'urry, sweet. I'd love to stay and linger a while." His smile left her in no doubt what he referred to. "To twist that knife just a little deeper for 'im.

Still, guess when 'e finds you – or bits o' you – it'll 'urt 'im just as much." Higgins stepped closer, a dreamy smile of his lips. "Been thinkin' I might send 'im a package a month. A little jar full of formaldehyde and maybe a tongue. Or an ear."

"That's if Rip hasn't found you yet." She glared back, forcing herself not to even think about the images his words conjured. If she gave into the terror turning her chest into a vice she'd start screaming and never stop. "That's why you're in such a hurry isn't it? Because you're afraid he'll find you."

Higgins's eyes narrowed. "Won't find me, pet. Buried the trail good an' proper." He touched her lips with the end of the hook. "Killed a lot o' me men, 'e did. Didn't take me seriously. Didn't consider me a threat." His words grew louder, eyes gleaming. "Now I'll show that mech-bastard and 'is master the error of 'is ways. Been watchin' I 'ave. Saw you two out a time or two. Saw you kiss 'im in the streets when I were plottin' me attack." He smiled. "Now we'll see which one of us ends up laughin'."

He grabbed one of the syringes. Esme strained but he managed to tear her sleeve with the hook and jerked a small leather tourniquet around her upper arm. The pain as it tightened made her vision swim. Blade had never been so rough with her when he used to use a tourniquet on her.

Esme screamed as Higgins pinned her ruthlessly with the pressure of the hook, sliding the needle into her vein with practiced ease. The sudden greedy suck of the machine filled the syringe vial in seconds, then blood spurted into the base of the enormous canister in the corner.

"No!" Her fingers were growing cold until he let the tourniquet go with a wrench. The sensation of the needle prickled at her, a cold sweat breaking out all over her skin. Esme was helpless to watch as he turned toward the tray to fetch another syringe.

A wordless roar echoed through the room. Esme's head jerked toward the door.

"John!" she screamed. "John!"

Her heart thundered to life in her chest and she yanked again. Her hand slipped a fraction further through the leather strap as Higgins moved toward the door.

"What the 'ell?" he snapped.

The door exploded inwards and Higgins flew backwards as a man was hurled through it. They both knocked over the tray of implements, the other man's neck twisted at an alarming angle.

Rip shouldered through the door, his black eyes locking on her. Esme's breath caught on a sob and she twisted against the restraints, tears blinding her.

"Be careful," she cried. "Please be careful."

Higgins came at him and Rip roared in fury again, grabbing the hook and burying it deep in the table in the corner. Higgins wrenched at it, his teeth bared, but the hook was stuck. Rip stepped forward and punched him, teeth and blood spraying everywhere.

Esme's arm was growing cold. She looked down at the tube and watched her blood being sucked toward the machine. "Hurry," she called.

Rip turned, his gaze locking on her arm. Then he was at her side, ripping the needle from her vein and pressing down on the tiny hole. Blood wet his fingers and Rip lifted his hand, staring at it with a breathless catch to his gasp.

"John," she whispered.

He blinked and pressed back down again.

"Watch out for the–"

Rip roared as something hit him from behind. His left knee gave way and he lashed out behind him as the hunchback dragged the knife out of his thigh and hefted it high again.

The hunchback flew across the room, smashing into the glass canister. Glass showered everywhere as he was impaled on a particularly sharp piece.

"No!" Higgins screamed, coming from the right and sinking the hook into Rip's side. The pair of them grappled, Rip staggering on his injured leg.

Esme yanked on the leather restraint, pain stealing her breath as her skin scraped and tore. Then her hand finally slipped free. She wasted no time, reaching for the other restraint and ripping the leather open.

Rip drove Higgins into the table and it splintered beneath the weight of them. Esme watched in horror as Higgins drove the hook high and buried it in Rip's back.

He'll heal, she told herself as she yanked at the straps around her feet. It was incredibly difficult to kill a blue blood. Still... It wasn't impossible.

Shoving off the table, she staggered against it as her head spun. Higgins lifted the hook again, Rip's hand clenched around his throat as he held him down. Esme didn't need to even think. She saw the cleaver on the floor at her feet and picked it up, hefting the weight in her hand like an old friend. This she knew.

Higgin's hook was just like a plucked chicken spread on her board. Esme lifted the cleaver high as the hook descended and cut through his arm to the bone.

Higgins screamed as blood sprayed across her face, warm and wet. The cleaver was stuck and Esme yanked at it, bile in her throat. Or perhaps not quite like a chicken. She swallowed hard and lifted it again, determined to complete the job. Her man was already injured. Nothing was going to hurt him anymore.

The cleaver cut through this time and the hook went sailing. All of the fight left Higgins and he thrashed and screamed until Rip yanked his neck sharply to the side.

Rip looked up as she staggered, "Jaysus."

His gaze locked on the cleaver and Esme dropped it with a shudder, her stomach heaving dryly. She couldn't look at the still twitching hook with its stump of bloodied arm. Instead, she caught Rip under the shoulder and eased him into a sitting position.

"Are you all right?" she whispered, watching the gleaming black drain out of his eyes.

Rip blinked down at himself, as if only just noticing his injuries. He probably was. Whilst in the grip of the craving, a blue blood was impervious to anything other than his intended target.

Esme examined his side, encouraging him to lean forward. Blood stained his shirt and the wound was closing sluggishly. "You haven't been drinking enough blood," she murmured. "This should have healed."

Taking a deep breath she reached for one of the razors still sitting on the tray on the floor.

"No." Rip caught her hand, shaking his head, his eyes black as night again. "No."

He was reeling however, blood loss and self-enforced deprivation making him weaker than he ought to be. Esme straddled his thighs, bringing the razor across her wrist in a sharp little motion that made her hiss between her teeth.

"You need it," she told him, bringing her wrist to his mouth.

Rip's nostrils flared and he tried half-heartedly to bat her hand away again. But the scent of her blood drew his gaze like a snake being hypnotised and suddenly he wasn't pushing her away anymore.

His lips locked over her wrist, a harsh moan filling the air. Esme gasped as his tongue swiped over her skin, the heat of it flooding through her body. Each sweet pull of his mouth was like a warm hand stroking between her legs. Lips parting, she rocked against him, straddling his thigh. "Yes," she whispered, feeling the burn deep within. "*Yes.*"

She could feel his heartbeat thumping against her like it was her own. Echoing the pulse between her thighs, igniting her blood until she felt like she was on fire.

Her fingers tingled, reminding her that he wasn't the only one who'd lost blood today. "Rip," she whispered. "You have to stop."

No matter how good this felt. How close to the edge she was. The little death, in all its reality. Esme bit her lip. "John!"

Rip gasped, shoving her hand away. Blood stained his lips and he licked them, looking up at her with those wicked-black eyes. His nostrils flared as if scenting the blood. "Cover it," he rasped hoarsely. "Before I can't stop meself."

Esme tore a strip off her skirt. The wound was already healing, courtesy of his saliva. Few thralls owned scars; only those who master's cared little enough to cleanse the wound afterwards or whose virus levels weren't strong enough. She would bear this one, she imagined, for she didn't dare ask him to lick it clean.

A sign of his mark on her body.

Forever.

Esme smiled and leaned her forehead against his, her body rising and falling with his breath. She cupped his face and kissed his lips lightly, tasting copper, sharp and sweet. "I knew you'd come," she whispered. "I knew all along that you'd come for me."

Rip kissed her hard. "Always, my love."

CHAPTER 12

*E*sme hummed under her breath as she diced a carrot, wielding the knife almost as easily as Rip could. Of course the way he used it was entirely different to her. Or perhaps not. Her smile faded as a flash of the cleaver thunking through solid bone hit her.

Weeks ago. But the memory was still as fresh as yesterday. And just as unsettling.

The door to the kitchen opened and Rip's eyebrow arched as she flinched, her fingers curling over the knife. He stomped his shoes in the doorway, getting rid of the snow and then tugged his collar high. Most of the snow had melted but last night had dropped one last white blanket across London.

He took in the spread of diced vegetables and lamb. "Shepherd's pie. Used to be me favourite." He rarely ate now; he didn't need to. Only bites sometimes, to savour the flavour.

"Used to be?" she asked with a smile as he wrapped his arms around her and dragged her back against the cradle of his chest.

"Mmm." Rip breathed in her scent, the rasp of his stubble roughening her neck. "I've a new favourite now."

Her. The thought thrilled her. Last night they'd shared another controlled blood-letting. He still drank most of his blood cold but it was becoming easier for him to control himself.

"You should come outside," he said. "Got somethin' to show you."

"I have to get dinner on." Still, she leaned into his embrace as his lips traced the side of her neck. "Perhaps... Perhaps just for a moment." A gasp, and then he let her go.

"Asked Lena to cook," he said. "You deserve an afternoon off and what I got to show you might take more than a moment."

Esme turned in his arms. "A present?"

A look of amusement softened the harshness of his face. "You're getting' greedy."

He'd been showering her with gifts ever since he'd gotten her back. Books he found in the markets, pieces of ribbon, a pair of mink gloves that must have cost him a small fortune... The gifts were overwhelming but Esme hadn't had the heart to chide him. She saw the pleasure he took in finding something to please her and knew that he'd never had that before. Someone to lavish his attention on. Warm arms that opened every time he turned to her. And a smile and kiss especially for him.

Her gentle giant. So fierce on the outside and strangely soft beneath.

"Show me," she whispered.

With an almost boyish smile, Rip slipped his mech fingers through hers and led her to the door. The gesture wasn't lost on her.

Outside the children were playing, Meggie watching wistfully from the stoop as Lark tripped Charlie facedown and shoved a handful of snow down the back of his shirt. He might be a blue blood now but Lark knew every dirty trick in the book. She laughed as Charlie cursed at her.

Skirting the yard, Rip led Esme to the old stables. "Turn around," he murmured.

"Why?"

A silk scarf untangled in his fingers and then he wrapped it across her eyes, effectively blindfolding her. The silk whispered over her skin. Esme sucked in a sharp breath as he knotted it behind her head. "John?"

"Trust me."

"Always," she admitted, letting him take her hand again. He led her forward and Esme hesitantly followed.

"There's a step," he murmured, trying to help her.

Esme's boots slipped on the edge and she stumbled. In the next second he'd swung her up into his arms.

"That's better."

"I agree," she replied, resting her fingertips against his chest. His heartbeat clipped along at a good pace. Strange. As though he was nervous.

The door clicked shut and Rip shoved the latch into place. Locking them in. Even through the sudden fall of darkness, Esme could sense something flickering. Perhaps candles.

"John, what are you up to?" she asked.

"You can take the blindfold off now," he said simply.

Esme tugged it free as he put her down, her eyes widening as she took in the room. It was transformed. All of the furniture was gone, replaced by a handful of tasteful carved pieces and a gold damask curtain that draped across half of the room, teasingly beckoning at something beyond. Hundreds of small candles had been placed in old jars and sprinkled everywhere, until she felt like she stood in the centre of a chandelier. They tracked over every available surface and a path of them led toward the curtain.

"What—What does it all mean?" she whispered, turning in circles and examining the room. It looked almost like a sitting room, with the old fireplace cleaned out and a pair of embroidered sofa's sitting on a rug.

"Thought we needed a place to ourselves," Rip said, one hand resting on the low-hanging beam overhead. He watched her carefully, as though trying to scrutinise her expression. "Yet it's close to the house, nice and safe. Just–" And here he stumbled, hints of red creeping up his cheekbones as his eyes dropped. "If you wanted. Thought the pair of us…"

The words trailed off. Rip took a deep breath.

"I love it," she said, still turning in small circles. She loved the Warren with all its hectic noise and laughter, but she had never had a place of her own. Somewhere just for them.

"You do?" He let out a relieved breath and followed her as she headed toward the curtain.

"What are you hiding behind here?" She yanked it back and stared at the enormous white cast-iron bed, with its pristine pink-and-white quilt and the mound of fluffy pillows. Candles trailed over the polished secretariat and the enormous copper bath in the corner. A new spigot gleamed in the wall. Hot water, just for her.

"'onoria 'elped me pick all the cushions and fripperies," Rip admitted.

"How the devil did you manage all of this without me knowing?" She took a step forward, trailing her fingers over the soft quilt. It was beautiful. Perfect. Candlelight blurred as happy tears flooded her eyes.

"Remember those times Lena took you shoppin' the last few weeks?" At her incredulous look, he laughed. "Blade and Will 'elped me with the 'eavy stuff. Tin Man too. Only when you weren't 'ere though."

The shopping trips. Traipsing through milliner's as Lena

prattled on, searching for the precise shade of cotton that she wanted for a dress. Cotton that never seemed quite the right colour.

"I can't believe you were all plotting against me," she said, spinning around again. The silk scarf dangled from her fingers. Esme glanced down, a soft smile dawning on her lips. "How could I ever thank you?"

Again his cheeks coloured. "You don't 'ave to thank me," he said gruffly. "I like makin' you smile."

Esme slid onto the edge of the bed, her velvet skirts whispering over the quilt. She patted the bed beside her. "Perhaps a kiss, to start with?"

Rip knelt on the bed, his hands clasping hers as he tumbled her onto her back. Esme stared up at him, candlelight warming his skin and gleaming in his beautiful green eyes. "I won't say no," he teased and leaned down to brush his lips against hers.

Aching sweet and just as tender. But it wasn't tender she wanted, not now. Her nails dug into the back of his hands as her fingers clenched, her thighs parting to welcome his weight atop her.

Rip drew back, breathing harshly. The obsidian glitter of his eyes reflected back a hundred candles. Esme slipped free of his grip, her arms sliding around his heavily muscled neck. Yanking his head down, she kissed him hard, stealing his breath, her tongue darting over his. His hips gave a teasing little flex, driving her into the feather-soft mattress.

Esme turned her face, kissing his cheek and nuzzling his ear. Her sharp little teeth worried at the fleshy lobe and he gasped, his hips thrusting hard, a sound almost of anguish stealing across his lips.

"You like that?" she whispered, licking the imprint of her teeth.

"Like it?" he shuddered. "I love it."

Esme put a hand to his shoulder and shoved. "Roll over."

He complied, landing flat on his back with her straddling him. The irony of seeing her fierce giant lying amid acres of fluffy white-and-pink cotton made her smile. Running her hands up under his coat, she slipped it over his shoulders, effectively trapping him.

"And now you're all mine," she whispered, leaning forward and untying the red scarf at his throat. Her nimble fingers darted over the buttons of his shirt and as each inch of tempting golden skin was revealed she licked it, nipping at his nipples and worrying them between her teeth.

"Esme." His hand slid through her hair, destroying her chignon. Not to push her away or pull her closer, but simply to hold her. As if he couldn't quite decide what to do.

She kissed his throat and then whispered into his ear, "I love you. All of you. Every wickedly delicious inch."

Rip's arms curled around her and he held her close, his body stiff, as if he couldn't quite believe the words. Esme seized the chance to slide her hand between them, her fingers darting under his waistband.

He sucked in a breath between his teeth. "Esme, I don't–"

"Shush," she whispered, her fingers closing over the silky-soft feel of him. So thick and firm. Throbbing beneath her touch. Wanting her so much that a slippery pearl of his seed gleamed wetly at his tip. She ran her thumb over it, again and again and Rip threw his head back with a groan.

"I'll stop if you can't control it," she whispered, "just let me please you."

His hand slid through her hair, trembling. Then he nodded.

Esme's tugged her fingers free and reached for the length of silk. "Hold onto the bed," she said. "I'm going to tie you up."

"Won't 'old me." Rough voice. Wicked eyes.

"I know. It's a reminder. So if you feel yourself approaching the edge, you might be able to pull yourself back." She ran the length of silk through her hands, her smile widening. "I think I quite like telling you what to do."

"Do you?" His eyes promised retribution.

"I do," she said with a challenging gleam in her eye.

Rip stared at her, then slowly reached back, the muscle in his biceps flexing and thin veins trailing up his arms. Esme leaned forward and swiftly tied his wrist to the bed. Then she used the other end to tie his mech hand down.

Slowly her hands crept to the buttons on her jacket. Rip watched with an intensity that made her shiver as she stripped herself out of her jacket and shirt.

The skirt took longer and required her to stand. Each layer slowly made a pool on the bed as she wiggled out of her under-skirt, camisole and bustle. Esme felt wicked as she slowly undressed, letting her hair out of its braids to tumble in loose waves down her back.

"Christ." Rip's eyes ate her up, his fingers curling into fists. "You're so beautiful."

And she felt it too, the way he looked at her. Wild and free and entirely sensual. Nobody's housekeeper or friend, but a lover, his gaze caressing her, as liquid as any touch.

"More," he whispered and her hands went to her hard metal busk of her corset.

She tugged it free until she wore only her shift and drawers. Then they too pooled around her ankles until she stood above him on the bed, her skin gleaming palely in the candle-light. She had a woman's body, lush and full, her belly rounded from sampling each dish she prepared. And he loved it. She saw his gaze lock on her breasts as she ran her hands up and over them, cupping their plump weight.

Breathing hard, Rip strained against the silk.

Esme straddled him, the dusky tips of her nipples begging

for his mouth. Rip licked one, the muscles in his neck straining. His teeth rasped over her, the hard pressure of his erection thrusting against her thigh. Esme moaned and worked her hands lower, tugging at his buttons until his cock jutted free. It spilled into her hands eagerly and Esme clenched her fingers, working his enormous length.

She loved watching him writhe beneath her, his eyes shut and his mouth parted as she wrung each gasp from him. Kneeling lower, she kissed his stomach, tugging his pants down over his hips. His boots hit the floor with a thud, then she stripped him of his pants and slid between his thighs. Rip watched her curiously and Esme flashed him a wicked smile.

Leaning down she took his erection in hand. "However can I thank you?"

"Esme," he growled in warning as she pumped her hand over him.

"Perhaps you'd like me to kiss you." Leaning down she pressed her lips against the smooth skin over his hips. "Here?"

Her only answer was the sound of his harsh breathing.

"Or perhaps here?" she asked, trailing her tongue across the groove of his hip and against the base of his balls. "No?" Looking up, she smiled at his dazed expression. "Where do you want me to kiss you?"

"You... know where..."

"Say it."

"My cock," he growled.

"John," she whispered in a shocked tone. "What a wicked man you are."

"Aye, I don't think I'm the only one who's wicked–"

The scalding heat of her mouth on him stole his breath, and his words. Esme took as much of him as she could, her tongue tracing lazy circles around the head of him.

"Christ, Esme." He shuddered, his erection thrusting past her lips. "Christ, you're the devil, woman."

Another gasp.

She worked him wetly, loving every moment of it. Watching him lose control, tugging unconsciously on his bonds. Desperate for her. Gasping. Cursing her.

She couldn't stop herself. She wanted more, wanted to feel him between her thighs. Sliding her hands up over his chest, she straddled him again.

"Esme." He threw his head back, spine arching and she was lost, aching so much she couldn't stop herself from rubbing her own secret wetness over him.

Rip hissed under his breath as the tip of his cock parted her. One hand tore free from the silk, then the other, hands clenching in the smooth flesh of her bottom. Thrusting her down until he buried himself to the hilt inside her.

Esme threw her head back and cried out. "Yes." Fingers curling into the hard muscle of his shoulder blades as he sat up. The action drove her down further until she was so full, too full of him.

His cool lips on her breast, teeth grazing, licking, suckling at her until she wanted to scream. She could barely move but he urged her on, hands kneading her bottom. Each glide of her hips ground her against him, the base of his shaft riding over the delicate flesh between her thighs until she shuddered. So close to breaking apart, to shattering completely.

"More," he growled.

But she could hardly move, she was trembling so much. "I can't—" Teeth sinking into her lip, she cried out as he rasped over her again.

Then she was tumbling onto her hands and knees as he spilled out of her and came to his knees behind her. Hands firming on her hips, he drove into her until Esme cried out in pleasure, her fingers curling in the quilt. So deep. As if he sought to bury his seed in her body.

A fist curled in her hair, dragging her up gently. She curved back against his body, her hips arching obscenely as he ran his mech hand over her stomach and up, cupping her breasts. The angle softened the impact of his thrusts. Then his other hand slid down, parting her curls and dipping wetly between her thighs.

"John," she whispered, sensation streaking through her. She pressed closer, wanting to feel every inch, his hard thigh muscles against the back of hers and fingers stroking her with cool possession. Knowing exactly where to touch, exactly what made her body tighten, liquid fire igniting in her veins.

Her man. All hers.

She came with a gasp, shuddering as his thrusts eased and he forced her to ride it out with exquisite slowness. Then she tumbled to her hands, unable to bear it any longer. "John, oh God, John."

Rip gripped her hips, thrusting long and hard. She could feel the tension in him, his fingers tight in the flesh of her bottom, as though he fought to hold on himself. And she didn't want that. She wanted him there with her, losing himself in the moment. Proving to himself that he could. Reaching back Esme cupped his balls, hearing his soft exhale as he thrust just a little harder, a little deeper.

Her body clenched around his, a wet, silken fist, as he shuddered and rode over something hot and sensitive inside her. Esme quivered, her body tightening again as her clever fingers played over him.

"Jaysus, luv." A gasp, torn from his lips. Her victory. Then he thrust harder, fingers digging in as she tightened further...

She cried out again, resting her forehead against her

forearm on the bed, feeling the shudder deep within as they both came. Panting, Rip collapsing over her... Somehow they disentangled and then she was in his arms as they tried to catch their breaths. Sweat slicked her skin, his seed wetting her thighs.

"Esme, you're wondrous." Rip kissed her shoulder, dragging her back into his arms. "So beautiful, so fuckin' tight." His stubble rasped her skin and she heard a soft laugh. As if he couldn't quite believe what had happened.

Rolling over, she rested her chin on his chest and smiled at him. A delicious shiver trailed down her spine as aftershock ran through her body. "You look eminently pleased with yourself."

Rip kissed her nose. "I am." He laughed. "Startin' to think I'd never 'ave you." His gaze sobered, voice going gruff. "Didn't 'urt you, did I? Can't judge me strength anymore."

"I believe I'm going to have fingerprint shaped bruises on my hips, but I survived." She smiled and kissed him. "I am made of sterner stuff than you believe."

"I know you are." His fingertips trailed over her cheek. "Do you think we made a babe?" he whispered, voice rough with unsuppressed desire.

"Would you like that?" she asked, a little hint of hesitation filling her.

They'd never spoken of it before but he had to know her feelings on the matter. She couldn't look at a child without feeling a pang of sweet sorrow deep inside. And Rip... he knew her so well. Sometimes she didn't have to even speak for him to know what she was thinking.

Except when it came to her feelings for him, of course.

She smiled and traced his mouth.

"Aye, I'd like it," he replied gruffly. One hand stroked over her hip with a tenderness that almost brought tears to her eyes. Then his smile widened; that wicked smile that always made her breath catch. The one only she ever got to see. "I guess I'll 'ave to see to it that I get you with child." He rolled over her, skating his fingertips over her sensitive stomach. "I'm fairly certain I'm up to the challenge."

Esme slid her hands over his shoulders. "I won't be a fallen woman, you know?"

"Aye, I know." He nipped at her shoulder. "Tryin' to ruin all o' me surprises, woman?"

"Surprises?"

He kissed her breasts, stubble rasping against her sensitive skin. "Under the bed, luv. I bought you another present to replace the one you lost. Figured this time I'd put it somewhere safer. Per'aps your finger, aye? This one?" Taking her left hand he drew it to his lips and sucked her ring finger into his mouth, watching her with those amused eyes.

Esme's breath caught. "Are you asking me to marry you?"

"Aye." His voice roughened in a growl. "I'm an old fashioned sort o' man. Ain't one of the Echelon with their consort contracts. I were born on the streets and 'ere on the streets, when a lad fancies a girl 'e asks 'er to be 'is alone."

Esme glanced toward the side of the bed. Her curiosity was rampant to see the ring and he knew it. "All yours then?"

"Mine," he agreed promptly. "If you'll 'ave me?"

She answered him with a kiss.

BEFORE YOU LEAVE THE LONDON STEAMPUNK WORLD

Dear Reader,

Thank you so much for reading! If you enjoyed *Tarnished Knight*, then get ready for *Heart of Iron*—when Lena finds herself in trouble, the only man who can help her is the hulking verwulfen lad who once spurned her kiss. Can she win Will's heart?

Complete series available now:

Kiss Of Steel
Heart Of Iron
My Lady Quicksilver
Forged By Desire
Of Silk And Steam

Novellas in same series:
Tarnished Knight
The Clockwork Menace

I hope we meet again between the pages of another book!

Cheers,
Bec McMaster

To win her heart, he'll have to win three challenges... But danger is lurking in the London streets.

When Caleb Byrnes receives an invitation to join the Company of Rogues as an undercover agent pledged to protect the crown, he jumps at the chance to find out who, or what, is behind a set of mysterious disappearances.

Hunting criminals is what the darkly driven blue blood does best, and though he prefers to work alone, the opportunity is too good to resist.

The problem?

He's partnered with Ingrid Miller, the fiery verwulfen woman who won a private bet against him a year ago. Byrnes has a score to settle, but one stolen kiss and suddenly the killer is not the only thing Byrnes is interested in hunting.

Soon they're chasing whispered rumours of a secret project gone wrong, and a monster that just might be more dangerous than either of them combined.

The only way to find out more is to go undercover among the blue blood elite...

ALSO BY BEC MCMASTER

DARK COURT RISING

Promise of Darkness

Crown of Darkness

Curse of Darkness

LEGENDS OF THE STORM SERIES

Heart Of Fire

Storm of Desire

Clash of Storms

Storm of Fury

Master of Storms

Legends of the Storm Boxset 1-3

COURT OF DREAMS SAGA

Thief of Dreams

Thief of Souls

Thief of Hearts

LONDON STEAMPUNK SERIES

Kiss Of Steel

Heart Of Iron

My Lady Quicksilver

Forged By Desire

Of Silk And Steam

Novellas in same series:

Tarnished Knight

The Clockwork Menace

LONDON STEAMPUNK: THE BLUE BLOOD CONSPIRACY

Mission: Improper

The Mech Who Loved Me

You Only Love Twice

To Catch A Rogue

Dukes Are Forever

From London, With Love

London Steampunk: The Blue Blood Conspiracy Boxset 1-3

DARK ARTS SERIES

Shadowbound

Hexbound

Soulbound

Dark Arts Boxset 1-3

BURNED LANDS SERIES

Nobody's Hero

The Last True Hero

The Hero Within

SHORT STORIES

The Many Lives Of Hadley Monroe

Burn Bright

ABOUT THE AUTHOR

BEC MCMASTER is a writer, a dreamer, and a travel addict. If she's not sitting in front of the computer, she's probably plotting her next overseas trip, and hopes to see the whole world, whether it's by paper, plane, or imagination.

Bec grew up on a steady diet of '80s fantasy movies like *Ladyhawke*, *Labyrinth*, and *The Princess Bride*, and loves creating epic, fantasy-based romances with heroes and heroines who must defeat all the odds to have their HEA. She lives in Australia with her very own hero, where she can be found creating the worlds of the London Steampunk, Dark Arts, Legends of The Storm, or Burned Lands series, where even the darkest hero can find love.

Read more at www.becmcmaster.com

THE END

Made in the USA
Las Vegas, NV
09 September 2021